Shea stared at the phone in her hand.

The voice Shea heard saying her name wasn't crisp *or* clear. It was barely audible.

"Shea Fallon?" the voice whispered.

"I can't hear you," Shea complained.

The whisper deepened, but it was still a whisper. *"Is this Shea Fallon?"*

"Yes," Shea said impatiently, "but can't you speak up? Who *is* this?"

"You don't have to worry," the whisper breathed. *"No one will know what you've done. I've seen to that."*

Shea stared at the phone in her hand. "What?"

"I said, don't worry. It's all taken care of. I'll let you know what I expect in return. Count on it."

Terrifying thrillers by Diane Hoh:

NIGHTMARE HALL

The Whisperer

DIANE HOH

SCHOLASTIC INC.
New York Toronto London Auckland Sydney

ISBN 0-590-48154-1

12 11 10 9 8 7 6 5 4 3 2   4 5 6 7 8 9/9

Printed in the U.S.A.   01

First Scholastic printing, June 1994

Prologue

The voice on the telephone was unrecognizable.

It was only a whisper. But not the soft, sweet whisper of a person in love. Not the soothing, comforting whisper of one friend to another. Not the conspiratorial, sly whisper of someone passing on gossip. Nothing so harmless as any of those.

This whisper was sinister, chilling, the voice low and threatening. It wafted through the wires like poisonous air, slithering out on Shea's end in a dark, sickening cloud, enveloping her in dread.

Because she had brought this on herself. And now she didn't know how to stop it.

This call was only the beginning, she knew that.

There would be others.

The whispers would continue.

Chapter 1

The conversation was hushed in one particular blue booth at Vinnie's Pizzeria, located in the village of Twin Falls, not far from Salem University. Comments were subdued, almost whispered, because the subject of the conversation sat only a few feet away, in an identical booth directly across the aisle.

Doctor Mathilde Stark, bane of science majors all across the beautiful, sprawling Salem campus, ate her fettucini Alfredo calmly, ignoring the whispers across the aisle. The tall, severely dressed professor sat hunched over an open textbook, apparently oblivious to the whispering group.

"Why does she wear her hair like that?" Dinah Lincoln, Shea Fallon's best friend, said. Dinah was short, plump, and easygoing, unlike Shea, who rushed through life as if she couldn't get enough of it. "It's almost the same color as yours, Shea. She would look much better if she wore it loose like yours. How *does* she get every hair to stay in place like that? Spray it with varnish?"

"She probably stared at it in the mirror with that evil eye of hers and *froze* it into place," Shea hissed balefully. But mixed with her anger was an overwhelming sense of guilt. If her friends knew what she'd done that very afternoon. . . . She couldn't tell them. Not even Dinah, who was the least judgmental person Shea knew. Even Dinah wouldn't understand or condone *this*. No way.

Well, why should she? Shea asked herself. *I don't condone it myself. I know it was a sleazy thing to do. But I had no choice. It was the only way.*

"I heard she mixes up a kettle of lethal brew and conjures up the ghosts of dead scientists whenever she needs to come up with a new, ever more terrifying exam," the large, blond boy sitting opposite Shea said in a low voice. Sidney Frye, Dinah's boyfriend, shared Dr. Stark's advanced biology class with Shea, as Dinah did.

A broad-shouldered girl in jeans and a Salem T-shirt, a mass of thick, golden hair spilling down her back, approached their table. The boy with her was tall, with dark hair and friendly gray eyes. He looked vaguely familiar to Shea. "You guys aren't being very subtle," the girl said. "I mean, all this whispering . . . you can't possibly be dumb enough to think Dr. Stark doesn't know you're raking her over the coals."

Shea groaned, "Tandy, you're my roommate. You know better than anyone what that woman has already done to me this year. How could it get worse? I'd never had a C in my life until I walked into that class. She hates me, that's all. I can tell by the way her upper lip curls in contempt when she returns my papers."

"That's ridiculous," Tandy Dominic said. She, too, was in the Advanced Biology Monday/ Wednesday/Friday nine A.M. class. "She's tough, but she's good. I've learned more from Dr. Stark this year than I've learned from all the other teachers I've ever had. You guys just don't try hard enough, Shea."

No one agreed with her.

Changing the subject, Tandy motioned toward the tall, dark-haired boy and said, "Shea, this is Cooper Doyle. Coop. He's in our bio class. I'm sure you've noticed him." A sly grin slid across her fair-skinned, oval face. "Because he noticed you . . ."

Cooper Doyle laughed. "Speaking of subtle," he said.

Tandy shrugged and tossed her hair. It fell around her shoulders in beautiful blonde waves. "Sorry. Subtlety isn't one of my fine points. Coop, meet Shea Fallon, my roommate."

When she had gone, Shea, her cheeks slightly pink, invited Coop to sit with them. She introduced him to Dinah, who surprised Shea by saying she already knew him. Coop worked with Sid, part-time, in the Animal Behavior Studies lab. Dinah often dropped in to see Sid while he was working, and had already met Coop there.

"You probably don't remember, but I ran into you earlier," he said to Shea as he slid into the booth beside her. "At Wilshire Hall. The science building?"

Shea almost gasped aloud. That was *him*? He remembered seeing her there? She had hoped, since she'd hurried away with only a breathless "excuse me," that he hadn't really had a good look at her.

Still . . . he couldn't know where she'd been rushing from, could he?

"So, do you enjoy that bio class as much as I do?" he asked with a grin. He, too, kept his voice low, aware of the professor sitting across the aisle.

If he knew what she'd been up to in the science building, he wouldn't be asking that question. She needed to get a grip on herself and answer him in as normal a tone of voice as possible, as if everything *were* perfectly normal.

If only it were . . .

"Maybe I should have taken regular freshman bio," Shea responded. "You know, the basics. But it sounded so boring. My advisor suggested that I take the advanced class instead, since I've never had any trouble in science. Until now. I didn't think it would be so tough."

"It's not," Sid said, keeping his voice low. "My roommate, Joe Cameron, has Professor Lambeth for bio, and he says it's a piece of cake. The problem isn't the subject, it's the *professor*," he grumbled, casting a sideways glance across the aisle. Then he shrugged his wide shoulders. "You just have to know how to deal with someone like that, that's all. Figure out what she wants, and give it to her."

Dinah smiled. "If you don't do well in her class, Sid, she'll fire you from your job at the Animal Behavior Studies lab, and then you won't have any more spending money. You'll never be able to take me out again."

Shea expected Sid to laugh, but he didn't.

The temptation then to confess all, to tell each of them what she had done was so overwhelming, Shea had to grab a slice of pizza from the tray and thrust it into her mouth, just to keep from blurting out the truth.

Fortunately, Dinah changed the subject then, mentioning in a normal voice an upcoming party at Nightingale Hall, an off-campus dorm.

Lost in thought as she chewed, Shea leaned against the back of the booth, not hearing Dinah's words. She still couldn't believe what she'd done. Never, not once in twelve years of school had she cheated.

You never *needed* to before, an inner voice pointed out bluntly. So don't be so sanctimonious about it. It wasn't that you were so noble. It was just that you always did well.

Obviously. Because now that she *wasn't* doing so well, what had she done? She'd cheated.

Well, not yet. She hadn't actually cheated yet.

But she'd laid the groundwork. Surreptitiously glancing across the aisle as Dr. Stark wiped her mouth with a paper napkin, picked up her check and her purse, and rose stiffly from her seat, Shea fought an irresistible urge to crawl under the table. She doesn't *know*, she told herself. She couldn't. She wasn't *there*.

That was true. Dr. Stark's office had been empty when, earlier that afternoon, Shea had tentatively turned the doorknob and opened the door a crack. If, over the wild beating of her own terrified heart, she had heard the slightest sound of activity inside the office, she would have ended it then. She would have turned around and raced down the hall and out the front door of Wilshire Hall. But she had heard nothing. The coast was clear.

As Dinah rambled on about the upcoming party, Shea replayed in her mind the scene from that afternoon.

She had never been so frightened in her life. She couldn't believe she was even contemplating cheating. But she was desperate. The scholarship that had sent her to Salem was an academic one, and had very strict demands. Nothing under a B, period. No negotiating there. A final grade of C in any subject meant that her mother would have to chip in some of her hard-earned savings to finance her daughter's education, something Shea knew her mother hadn't counted on doing. The relief in Mrs. Fallon's face last July at news of the full-tuition scholarship had been undisguised.

But Fiona Fallon's darling daughter had as much chance of earning anything above a dis-

mal D in Dr. Stark's deviously devised exam tomorrow morning as she did of being elected president. No way.

Unless . . . unless she had a copy of the exam. . . .

She had fought the idea. She knew plenty of kids in high school who had done it. But she'd never even had to think about it then. And she'd been awfully judgmental, it seemed to her now, about the kids who had. Miss Superior. Miss Self-Righteous. Saint Shea.

Now, she understood. She could not flunk that exam tomorrow. She had studied and studied, until her eyes were crossed and her brain felt like mush, but she knew she still wasn't ready for Dr. Demento's worst.

She couldn't believe the door to Dr. Stark's office was unlocked, the office empty when Shea peered inside. Wasn't that kind of unsafe? Dr. Stark must be a lot more trusting than she looked. Most of the time, she acted like students were the lowest form of life on the planet. She clearly wasn't one of those teachers who believed in being "pals" with her students. So why the open-door policy?

Biting her lower lip, Shea peered around the corner of the office door. No one in sight. Was the exam even in the office? Would Dr. Stark be that careless?

If she'd only stepped out for a minute, she might have left the exam on her desk.

Hurry, hurry! Shea urged herself, stepping into the room, closing the door behind her. She didn't dare lock it. If the good doctor showed up, an excuse could be invented for being there, but there'd be no excuse for having locked the door.

Breathing in tiny, panicky gasps, Shea ran to the huge, antique desk of dark wood, pushing aside the thick fronds of a tall, potted plant stationed beside it, and began fumbling through a thick pile of papers. The soft hum of a humidifier sitting on the floor beneath the radiator and the rhythmic tick-tock of a round wooden wall clock were the only sounds in the bright, neat room filled with hanging plants and attractive colonial furniture. Shea couldn't help noticing that the room seemed far more warm and welcoming than the woman who occupied it. Maybe someone else had decorated it.

The next few minutes were nightmarish. Thumbing frantically through the pile of papers, she sliced a finger on a crisp sheet of paper, leaving a thin trail of red on the next few sheets. When she realized that she was leaving "evidence" of her visit, she was horrified. She took a confused step backward, stumbling into the potted plant. Her left elbow struck the heavy green desk lamp, knocking it to the floor and taking with it a large, cube-shaped, copper paperweight. Shaking, Shea bent and picked up both objects and set them back on the desk. Then she wrapped a tissue around the injured finger before returning to the pile of papers.

She found the exam after a few more moments of frenzied searching. It was dated. Tomorrow's date. No question about what it was.

There was no answer sheet accompanying the exam. Didn't matter. With the questions in her possession, she could look up the answers in her textbook.

She didn't dare steal the test. Pointless. If she walked off with it, there wouldn't be a test. When Dr. Stark discovered the exam was missing, she'd wait until she'd composed a new and different one. And this risky visit to the professor's office would become a wasted effort.

Copy . . . she needed a copy of the test. But how . . . ?

A computer and printer were stationed off to her left. The exam had almost certainly been written on the word processor and then printed. The printer was a laser . . . very fast. But she didn't know the file name. Without it, she couldn't call up the exam and print her own copy.

Would a teacher who had a quick, efficient printer also have a copy machine? Probably not. She could simply print extra copies directly off the word processor.

The tick-tock of the wall clock hammered in Shea's ears.

So frightened she felt physically ill, she clutched the exam and glanced around the room. There was a smaller room off to one side, its door standing open. She had glanced inside when she entered the office to make sure no one was in there. But she hadn't really checked it out.

She hurried over to peek inside a second time.

And there it was, big as life, a copy machine, standing against the wall, already loaded with paper.

Shea glanced back toward the office door again, her eyes wide with apprehension. She was taking a terrible chance. Any second now, Dr. Stark could burst into the office. When she saw Shea with a copy of the exam in her hands, her eyes would narrow and turn icy blue, and she would say in that brittle voice of hers, "Ms. Fallon? What exactly is it that you're doing in my office and what is that in your hands?"

And my life will be ruined totally and forever, Shea thought, clenching her teeth.

But she couldn't turn back now. She had the exam in her hands. It was only four pages, and unless the copy machine was a relic from the dark ages, it would only take a few seconds to copy the entire exam.

She had to do this. She had to.

The seconds that it took to copy the exam were the longest of Shea's life. The machine was fast, quiet, and efficient. But while it was copying, her ears strained for the sound of footsteps and her hands trembled so that she could barely lift the finished pages out of the tray.

Then it was done. All four pages, neatly printed, were in her hands. She held them tentatively, as if she expected them to burst into flames at any moment.

Still, not having the answer sheet seemed to make her deed less dastardly. Maybe you weren't really cheating if you didn't steal the answers.

A sound from outside in the hall froze her in her tracks. She held her breath.

But no one entered the office.

She turned off the copier and ran back into the outer office, where she hurriedly thrust Dr. Stark's copy of the exam into the pile of papers on the desk. Then she opened the door carefully, peering out to see if the hallway was clear.

It was.

Sliding the papers inside her blue cardigan, Shea slipped out of the office, closed the door behind her, and hurried down the hall. No running . . . too obvious. But she walked quickly. Rounded a corner and . . .

Ran headlong into the tall, dark-haired guy who was now sitting beside her.

She couldn't remember exactly what she had said or what he had said . . . she had a vague impression of having mumbled "excuse me" and clutching the front of her cardigan to keep the exam copy hidden. It felt as if it were burning right through the fabric. He had, she thought now, smiled and backed away. If he had said anything, she'd been too frazzled to comprehend it.

Remembering how easily she could have given herself away, Shea shuddered as she swallowed the last of her pizza.

"What?" Coop, sitting beside her, asked. "Somebody just walk over your grave?" He smiled as he said it. He had a lean look about him, no fat anywhere. She wondered if he was an athlete.

No, no one walked over my grave, Shea thought. But maybe I just walked all over my own future.

Too late now. She would have to keep telling

herself she'd had no choice. Maybe eventually she'd even believe it.

Coop and Sid went off to play pool in the back room. Dinah went to the ladies' room, and Shea was about to follow her when one of the waiters called out her name. "Phone!" he added, pointing toward a little alcove off to one side.

Phone? Here? Tandy, maybe?

But when Shea said hello into the wall phone tucked away in the short, dark corridor, it wasn't Tandy's voice that greeted her. Tandy's voice was crisp and clear and confident.

The voice Shea heard saying her name wasn't crisp *or* clear. It was barely audible.

"Shea Fallon?" the voice whispered.

"I can't hear you," Shea complained.

The whisper deepened, but it was still a whisper. *"Is this Shea Fallon?"*

"Yes," Shea said impatiently, "but can't you speak up? Who *is* this?"

"You don't have to worry," the whisper breathed. *"No one will know what you've done. I've seen to that."*

Shea stared at the phone in her hand. "What?"

"I said, don't worry. It's all taken care of. I'll let you know what I expect in return. Count on it."

Chapter 2

"What did you say?" Shea asked, her own voice a mere whisper.

Click. The line went dead.

"Hey, you okay?" a waitress passing by asked. "You look like that red hair of yours is about to turn white."

"I'm okay," Shea mumbled, turning away to replace the telephone. She was trembling. Someone knew what she'd done that afternoon?

No . . . no, it couldn't be. How *could* anyone? No one had seen her going into or coming out of Dr. Stark's office. Only Cooper Doyle had seen her in the hall and he couldn't have known where she was coming from. There were so many other offices . . .

But . . . what *else* could the telephone call have meant? Stealing the exam was the only thing she'd tried to get away with. It wasn't like she was a hardened criminal. No long list of illegal activities for her to sort through, trying to find the one uncovered by the caller. There was only this one thing.

How could someone *know*?

Her hands were shaking so violently she had to stuff them into the pockets of her navy blue cardigan. Leaving the alcove, she hurried back to the booth and sank down on the seat. She was grateful that none of the others had returned yet. If they saw her like this, they'd know something was up.

And what would you tell them, Shea? she asked herself. You'd have to make something up. See how one crime leads to another?

Lying isn't a crime, she argued silently. If it were, no one would be left on the streets. Everyone would be in jail.

She took a sip of water in an effort to compose herself. She had to pull herself together before the others returned. Except for her romance with Sid, which Shea didn't understand, Dinah was very perceptive. It was going to be hard to hide a guilty conscience from her.

Another sip, and Shea felt a little better. Whoever that had been on the phone, they couldn't possibly know what she'd done. The whispering voice had to be talking about something else. Maybe some girl who had a crush on Cooper Doyle had seen him sitting with her and had flipped out with jealousy.

"Excuse me," Shea called out to a waiter, "but is there another phone in here? Besides the one in that little alcove, I mean?"

He pointed. "There's a pay phone up front," he said. "By the door." He hurried away.

A pay phone. So someone in *here* could have called her from the telephone in front. Some girl who was jealous, watching her talking to Coop . . .

Reality check here, an inner voice said with contempt. You know perfectly well that call referred to the stolen exam. You just don't want to believe someone knows.

"What's wrong?' Dinah asked even before she'd slid into the booth.

I knew it, Shea told herself. I knew she'd notice. "Nothing. I'm beat, though. And," willing herself not to flush guiltily, "I've got that bio exam. I'm leaving. You coming?"

"Aren't you going to wait for the guys?" Dinah grinned. "I think Coop wants to get to know you better. Not that you need another guy in your life. It's not like your social calendar is empty. You haven't spent a weekend night in your room since you got here. But I think Coop has potential."

Just then Coop and Sid emerged from the back room. Shea didn't like Sid. She'd never figured out what Dinah saw in him. They'd been together since high school, so maybe Sid was just a hard habit for Dinah to break. He wasn't bad-looking, but he was cynical and sarcastic, often openly critical of Dinah in front of others. Shea hated that. She didn't understand it. Dinah deserved better.

Go figure, she thought as Sid put a careless arm around Dinah's shoulders. He was far too proprietary for Shea's tastes, resenting it whenever Dinah wanted to do something with her friends. Dinah didn't seem to mind as much as Shea did.

"Any reason why we can't all walk back to campus together?" Coop asked lightly, his eyes on Shea.

Not if you don't mind walking with a cheat, she thought. If he only knew. . . . Not one of the three of them would believe it if she told them. Not Miss Self-Righteous, who gets so indignant about little injustices, like when Dinah got a speeding ticket from the campus police for going only five miles over the speed limit, or when Tandy had to pay an extra fee because someone in the bursar's office lost a check she'd given them.

There I was, Shea thought miserably, yelling and hollering, "That's not right! That's just not right! It's the principle of the thing!"

She was a fine one to judge what was right and what wasn't.

Tired of being disgusted with herself, she forced a smile and nodded at Coop. "No reason at all," she said casually. "We're all going in the same direction, right?" He seemed nice enough and she liked the way his eyes smiled even before his mouth did. Besides, she told herself as they left Vinnie's, even condemned prisoners get a last meal. Maybe I'm entitled to a last fling with a cute guy. Before my life turns to ashes.

It was odd, walking up the road toward campus with someone who talked casually and easily about college life, as if everything were perfectly normal. As, of course, it was . . . to *him.* *He* was on his way back to his dorm to study for the bio exam. But she was going back to study a copy of an exam she had *stolen.*

Trying desperately to have a good time, Shea forced from her mind the grim thought that nothing was normal for her now. Maybe it never would be again.

The telephone whisper slithered through her mind. *"It's all taken care of."*

What did that *mean?*

Wishing her luck on the test, Coop left her

at the door to Devereaux Hall. He lived in the Sigma Chi house, and he and Sid turned in that direction.

"He's nice," Dinah commented as they prepared to part at the door to Dinah's room, five doors down the fourth-floor hall from Shea's.

Caught off guard Shea said, "Who?"

Dinah laughed as she opened the door. "Boy, that exam really has you tied up in knots! I meant Coop. Don't you think he's nice?"

Yeah, she did. So what? Romance wasn't on her agenda just now. "Yeah, I guess so. He seems okay."

Dinah laughed. "Just okay? Tandy wanted him for herself, couldn't you tell? She'd be pretty ticked off if she heard you playing it so cool about him." As she went inside, she said, "Good luck tomorrow in Stark's class. I'll keep my fingers crossed."

"Thanks." As the door closed, Shea felt a pang of envy. Dinah didn't have to worry about the exam. Which was why she wouldn't understand Shea's desperation.

If Tandy had been in their room on Devereaux's fourth floor, Shea would have been forced to go to the library to study, afraid that Tandy would catch a glimpse of the exam copy. But Tandy was out. Maybe at Nightingale Hall again, the off-campus dorm where one of Tandy's best friends and swim teammate, Linda Carlyle, lived. Tandy sometimes stayed overnight with Linda, especially if they had an early-morning practice or were going on the road to a meet.

Shea shivered. She didn't understand how Tandy could sleep in that place. Nicknamed Nightmare Hall because of its gloomy appearance and rumors of strange things happening there, it was a huge, tired old house sitting high up on a hill off the highway, surrounded by deep, dark woods, its wide front porch tilted slightly. The shade of giant oak trees turned its worn red brick almost black. Shea had never had any trouble believing the stories about Nightmare Hall. From the outside, at least, it looked like something out of a horror movie.

Tandy shrugged away the stories. "I like it up there. It's fun."

Fun? Maybe. If you had a thing for bats and spiders and the wind howling through cracks in the walls. The Addams Family would be right at home there.

Tandy didn't come back that night. She called to say she was staying over with Linda, which left Shea free to openly study the copy of the exam. Just to be on the safe side, she locked the door.

She studied all night long. By morning, aided

by the exam copy and her textbook, she thought she had soaked up enough information to pull at least a B on the bio exam. *If* she could stay awake in class after being up all night.

But before she left for class, she used scissors to dice the exam copy into microscopic pieces and flushed them down the toilet.

When Dr. Mathilde Stark walked into the room, her mouth was pulled into a stern, straight line.

"Uh-oh," Dinah whispered to Shea, "fasten your seat belt."

The professor stood front and center in the large, square room. "Ladies and gentlemen," she began in a chilly voice, "I wish to call your attention to the fact that I did not fall off a turnip truck yesterday."

There were giggles and titters in the classroom.

"When I leave an exam on my desk and my office door unlocked," the professor continued, "I do it for a reason. I am well aware that in this modern age of strong ambition and weak scruples, the temptation may be greater for some than for others."

Shea stopped breathing.

"I wish to weed out those weak links. They have no business on a college campus. Hard work is the only way to achieve an education, and that will never change. Furthermore, I do not wish to lock my door when I am out of my office briefly, and I see no reason to keep my teaching materials under lock and key. I shall continue these practices as long as I draw breath. That is not only my preference, it is my right."

She knows, Shea told herself with a growing sense of horror. She *knows*.

"In my pursuit of those weak-kneed fools who refuse to earn a grade by simple hard work and study, I have chosen to take advantage of this age of technology. I recently took the precaution of installing the latest in technological advances — the videocamera — in my office."

Shea's head began to throb.

"I should like to point out," Dr. Stark added, beginning to pace back and forth in front of her captive audience, "that I took this measure four days ago. That is *four*, ladies and gentlemen. The camera has been operative ever since." The skirt of her dark, long-sleeved dress slapped at her booted ankles as she walked and talked. "Now, I might add that I am particularly anxious to view the film from yesterday afternoon, as I have reason to believe that the exam which you are about to take has been viewed by eyes other than mine."

Shea's head swam. Videocamera? Film?

Of *her?*

Yes. Of *her.* The thief in question.

"If I am right," Dr. Stark concluded with a cold, sly smile as she began to hand out exam papers, "a star has been born in the cinema filament. Perhaps, if the quality of the film is acceptable, we shall all view it in this room on Monday morning at this same hour." Then she added with mocking glee, "Wouldn't *that* be fun?"

Under her desk, Shea's knees knocked against each other. She was on film, stealing a test? The entire class was going to get to watch her sneaking around her science teacher's office? Filching the test from that pile of papers on the desk? Copying it? Dr. Stark was going to show her criminal act . . . in *class?*

She wouldn't. She *couldn't.*

Oh, but she could. Would. Of course.

The humiliation wouldn't end there. There would be serious repercussions. Salem University's honor code was sternly enforced. Cheating meant automatic expulsion.

What had she been *thinking* of? Why had she done it? She had worked her buns off to get to college, and now it was all going to end after only one-and-a-half semesters.

She *had* to stop Dr. Stark from showing that incriminating film.

Chapter 3

Shea lingered in her seat until everyone else had gone, telling Dinah not to wait for her. She had to confess to Dr. Stark. Had to throw herself on the professor's mercy. Crawl on her hands and knees if necessary. And the sooner she did, the better.

Still, she didn't get up. Her legs felt like water. She sat at her desk in the empty room while the teacher collected her briefcase and papers and moved out from behind the lectern.

Now! Shea ordered. Get your cowering self down there before she leaves . . .

A student appeared in the doorway. "Phone call for you, Dr. Stark," the boy said.

"I'll take it in my office," the professor replied, and hurried out of the room.

Shea groaned. She'd blown it. Wimp! she thought with contempt. Now you'll have to face the lion in its den. You'll have to go back into that office and face her there.

Still she didn't get up. She didn't know how long she sat there, but eventually she became aware that many minutes had passed, and pulled herself to her feet. Reluctantly, feeling as if she were headed for a gallows, she left the bio room.

Up two flights of stairs, down the hall, around a corner . . . there it was, the office she had entered yesterday, a thousand years ago. With the door shut, it looked like any other office.

Maybe they'll install a plaque over the door, Shea thought as she forced her watery knees forward. It'll say, THIS IS WHERE SHEA FALLON MET HER DOOM.

Knock, she ordered herself. Don't just burst in there like a fool. Knock first. Maybe she'll give you points for good manners.

As if that would help. As if Dr. Stark would be swayed by an impressive show of etiquette.

Well, you never knew. A little ordinary courtesy *could* soften her up.

Shea knocked.

No answer.

She knocked again, harder this time.

No response.

She tried the doorknob and was amazed to

find it moved. The door wasn't locked.

Just like yesterday, Shea thought angrily. Does the woman never learn? If the door had been locked yesterday afternoon, the way it *should* have been, none of this would be happening.

It felt good to shift the blame to someone else.

Shea pushed the door open. "Dr. Stark? Are you in here? It's Shea Fallon. From your nine o'clock advanced bio class?"

The only sound she heard was the familiar, maddening *tick-tock* of the wall clock.

There was no tall, stern professor seated behind the big wooden desk.

The desk . . . there was something wrong with the desk.

Shea took a step forward.

All of the neat piles of paper were in disarray, as if all of a sudden, a strong wind had ripped through them. And the lamp was gone, the green banker's lamp that had tangled her in its cord yesterday.

Shea studied the top of the desk. Where was the heavy copper cube? The paperweight?

Someone had made a mess of Dr. Stark's things.

Shea's heart thudded. The mess looked *angry*, as if someone had swept a furious arm across the top of the desk. She glanced around the room, and then her eyes went to the door leading to the copy room. Was that angry person still here, in the office? Hiding, maybe?

She listened.

Holding her breath, she tiptoed through the larger office toward the copying room.

She kept going until she reached the open door.

Tick-tock, tick-tock . . .

The room was unoccupied. The copy machine was still there, and the couch, but nothing . . . or no one . . . else.

Shea hesitated. It had taken so much energy to summon up enough courage to confront the professor. Now, she'd have to go through that process all over again. And if she left now and went to her other scheduled classes, who knew when she might catch the professor in? It wasn't as if she had all the time in the world. This was something that had to be handled *now*. Before Dr. Stark strolled on over to the administration building and the Dean, with that disastrous bit of film in her hot little hands.

Should she just plop down on the couch and wait?

No. Bad idea. If Dr. Stark came back and found someone she probably already knew to be a cheat hanging out there and her desk in a mess, she'd assume Shea was responsible.

I'll wait out in the hall, Shea decided. That way she can't accuse me of anything . . . anything besides what I've *already* done.

Maybe she wasn't even on that film. Maybe the camera had malfunctioned.

And maybe Dr. Stark is the sweetest, most generous person alive, Shea thought cynically, turning and aiming for the outer office door.

That was when she saw it. Sticking out from the far end of the desk, opposite the door. There was a smaller potted plant at this end of the desk. The plant, Shea realized, wasn't real.

But the foot she was looking at *was*.

A foot . . . in a black leather ankle-high boot, the hem of a dark-printed skirt lying against it.

Shea stood perfectly still. *Tick-tock, tick-tock.*

"Dr. Stark?" she whispered tentatively. After a moment or two of silence broken only by the ticking of the clock, she repeated the name, louder this time. "Dr. Stark?"

She knew then that she hadn't really expected an answer. Hadn't she already guessed that something was very, very wrong?

I can't go over there, she thought, knowing even as she thought it that she had no choice.

She *had* to walk over to look behind the desk. She couldn't just *leave*, even though every nerve in her body was screaming at her to do just that.

Biting on her lower lip, Shea walked slowly, fearfully, over to the desk. Taking a deep breath and slowly exhaling, she bent forward to peer around it.

And groaned aloud, one hand flying to her mouth, her knees buckling. She slid to the floor and then quickly scuttled backward until she her spine slammed into a chair. She sat there, her eyes wide with disbelief, staring.

Mathilde Stark was sprawled awkwardly, arms and legs akimbo, on the hardwood floor. She was lying facedown, her head turned away from Shea. Her reddish-brown hair had fallen free of its customary bun and spilled across her shoulders. A quarter-sized splotch of bright red stood out vividly on the back of her skull, with a matching splotch at her right temple. More red spilled out across the beige carpet beneath her.

She looks younger unconscious, Shea thought numbly, all of her senses frozen. Not that Dr. Stark was all that old. It was the way she dressed, in those dark, plain clothes, and the way she wore her hair, skinned back from her face like that, that made it hard to guess her age.

But she certainly wasn't old enough to *die*.

Shea snapped out of it, then. If the professor was still alive, she would need help.

The first thing was to find out if she was breathing. That meant *touching* her. Shea felt sick. But it had to be done and she was the only one there, although she could no longer remember exactly *why* she was there.

Crawling on her hands and knees, she made her way over to the body sprawled between the desk and the taller potted plant. The hand that reached out to check a limp wrist was trembling wildly.

The limp wrist had a pulse.

Dr. Stark was still alive.

But for how long?

Shea sank back on her haunches. And noticed then, the lamp and the copper paperweight, both lying on the floor above the professor's head, a few papers scattered between them. If either the lamp or the paperweight had struck her, no wonder she was unconscious and bleeding. They were both very heavy.

Shea, moving in a stunned fog, got up then and reached for the telephone on the desk.

She gave the location and Dr. Stark's name to the emergency services dispatcher. But when she was asked for her name, she gasped and slammed down the phone. It had suddenly occurred to her that she could *not* be found in this room.

She was almost certainly on that videotape. Dr. Stark had announced to the entire class that she had caught someone cheating and that she intended to share with them the incriminating evidence. And then Dr. Stark had been attacked somehow, probably hit on the back of the head with something heavy. The paperweight?

And here was Shea Fallon, one of the professor's students and possibly the star of an incriminating videotape, standing in this room at the very moment when Dr. Stark lay unconscious and bleeding on the floor.

The trouble I was in five minutes ago, before I entered this office, Shea thought dismally, was nothing compared to the trouble I'll be in if I'm found in this room now.

It wasn't as if she could help the victim. What did she know about first aid? Nothing. The woman needed paramedics, a doctor, a nurse. Not a terrified, shaking basket-case.

I've done everything that I can, Shea told herself as she began a hasty retreat. I've called for help. They'll come and find her and take care of her. I don't need to be here when they come.

But at the last moment, she ran back into the smaller room and grabbed an old afghan from the back of the leather couch and tossed it over Dr. Stark. Didn't people always do that in movies when someone was hurt?

She heard a siren shrieking in the distance, approaching Wilshire Hall.

Taking one last, guilty look at the body on the floor, Shea turned and ran from the room.

Chapter 4

Terrified that she would run into someone in the elevator or the halls, Shea took the fire stairs, two at a time, down to the first floor. She knew she must look frightening. Her skin had to be as white as marble, she was unsteady on her feet, her eyes bulging. They might not think much of it now . . . a fight with a boyfriend, a bad grade? . . . but later, when they heard about Dr. Stark, they'd put two and two together and get . . . well, what they'd get could spell disaster for Shea Fallon.

She laughed aloud, a cold, hollow sound echoing throughout the dim, deserted stairwell. As if she weren't already swimming in disaster, and with no help from anyone. She'd done that all by herself.

But as long as no one had seen her running from Dr. Stark's office this afternoon, there was still a remote chance that she wouldn't drown.

Then she remembered the phone call at Vinnie's. If someone knew about the stolen exam, her chances of getting out of this mess weren't remote . . . they were nonexistent.

Still, as if it were a life preserver, she clung to a tiny shred of hope that the call hadn't meant anything. She would cling to it tenaciously until every last trace of hope was gone.

I shouldn't be thinking about myself now, she thought in disgust as she reached the outside rear door and heard the nearby wail of a siren. She waited at the door until the siren abruptly ceased and a door slammed, then another.

The help she had summoned for Dr. Stark had arrived.

Had they arrived in time?

She wouldn't know that until later. How was she going to get through those minutes, maybe hours, until she knew for certain that the professor was okay? She wouldn't even be able to ask anyone, at least not until the word got around campus.

That wouldn't take long. News like that sailed around campus faster than a balloon escaping from a small child's hand. Someone would hear the siren and run downstairs to see what was up. Soon the story would be sailing out over the tall, wide, brick buildings, over the Commons, the dorms, the stadium and the football field, over the huge white-pillared fraternity and sorority houses, until every person on campus had heard the story.

But the story won't say *how* it happened, or *why* it happened, or even exactly *what* happened, Shea thought grimly as she slipped out of the rear door and hurried across campus toward Devereaux. No one, including me, knows the answers to any of those very important questions. Not yet.

"Hey, where're you headed?"

Shea was so lost in her own miserable thoughts, she stumbled and would have fallen if a hand hadn't grabbed her elbow.

Sid. Sid Frye, Dinah's boyfriend, smiling down at her with that sardonic grin, as if he knew exactly what she'd been up to.

She knew it was important to speak in a normal voice, act normally. It took every ounce of self-discipline she possessed. "Oh, hi, Sid. Thanks for the save. I guess I was out in space. I'm on my way back to the dorm."

"I'm headed that way, too. I need to see Dinah. How'd you do on the exam?" His eyes were so dark, they reminded her of marbles.

They had that same cold emptiness. What did warm, funny Dinah see in him?

Shea shrugged. "Okay, I guess." Liar! But talking about Dr. Stark's test might lead to talking about Dr. Stark herself, and Shea couldn't do that. Not now. She might do something stupid and revealing, like burst into tears. Sid must have heard the siren, and he wasn't stupid. He'd make the connection, sooner or later. "So," she managed in a casual tone, "where are you and Dinah off to?"

"Did I say we were going anywhere? I just need to talk to her, that's all. Any objections?"

He knew how Shea felt about him. Dinah had told him. And then had confessed to Shea, saying, "Sid doesn't understand why. He's never done anything to you." True. But he treated her best friend as if he owned her, and that, Shea couldn't fogive. It amazed her that Dinah tolerated it.

Ever since Dinah had told Sid how Shea felt about him, he'd continually baited Shea, trying to get a rise out of her. She'd thought for some time now that what he was hoping for was a full-blown argument, forcing Dinah to take sides. That was how sure he was that Dinah would choose *him*, leaving Shea out in the cold.

"No," she said flatly. "Why would I object?" Fighting with Sid now was a luxury she couldn't afford. Not with everything else crashing in around her.

Giving up, Sid said casually, "You hear the ambulance?"

"I heard a siren," Shea said, thinking that the late-springtime sun was awfully hot. Its rays blinded her, made her think of an overhead light in a police station, glaring down upon a prisoner while interrogators urged him to confess. "I thought maybe it was a fire truck or the police. How do you know it was an ambulance?"

"Saw it. Passed me. It went to Wilshire." His thin lips creased in a humorless smile. "I suppose it's too much to ask that maybe some evil befell Brunhilda Stark. The gods are not that generous."

Guess again, Shea thought, and willed herself not to shudder. Sid Frye was, by nature, a suspicious person. One wrong signal from her and his antennae would spring to attention.

She fell silent, then, no longer willing to make the effort to play it cool. She felt frail and frightened inside, and marvelled that Sid couldn't see that. Her nerves were screaming. The soft, gentle rustle of the pale pink dogwood blossoms overhead set her teeth on edge, so that she was unable to respond to countless "Hi, Shea"s that came her way as they walked across the thick green grass toward Devereaux Hall.

By the time they reached the tall, red-brick dorm, she felt completely drained. When they got upstairs, she was going to take a long hot shower and try to pull herself together.

But when she got to her room, Dinah was waiting in the hall.

The minute Shea saw her face, she knew she was not going to have the luxury of waiting until she felt stronger to share the bad news about Dr. Stark. Dinah already knew. It was written all over her round, tanned face. Her dark brown eyes were wide with shock.

It's bad, Shea thought as her heart slid into her shoes, it's very bad.

"I just heard," Dinah began, "Dr. Stark . . . she . . . she was attacked in her office. Someone cracked her on the head. She's in the hospital. Not the infirmary."

Shea knew what Dinah meant. Minor injuries were taken to the campus infirmary. So Dr. Stark's head wound had been far more serious than it had looked.

Shea had to bite her tongue to keep from crying out, "No, it wasn't that bad! There were just these two small places where her head was bleeding," as if by denying the severity of the damage, she could also deny her part in it.

That thought surprised her. Her part in it? She *had* no part in what had happened to Dr. Stark. What a weird thing to think! She had tried to help the professor. Called the ambulance, tossed a blanket over her. That's all she'd done.

So, why did she feel so guilty?

"How do they know she was attacked?" Shea asked, staying where she was in the middle of the hall. If she moved closer, Dinah might see something in her face, in her eyes . . . "Maybe she just fell, hit her head on those big bookshelves behind her desk."

Dinah shook her head. "I heard Dr. Stark was conscious when the emergency people got there. She told them something was missing. A heavy copper paperweight. The campus police think it was the weapon, and that the attacker took it with him. The Twin Falls police are being called in. Isn't it awful?"

Shea almost blurted out, "That paperweight isn't gone! It was there a few minutes ago, when I . . ." She stopped herself just in time. She felt dizzy with confusion. How could the paperweight be gone? It had been there . . . she had *seen* it. Now, it was gone?

Realizing what must have happened, she shuddered with fear. Dr. Stark's attacker had returned to get the incriminating paperweight, probably only seconds after Shea had run from the office. She'd missed him by a hair.

"Fingerprints," Sid said knowingly. "If that's what she was hit with, there'd be fingerprints on it. That's why the attacker took it."

Fingerprints? Shea sucked in her breath. In her mind, she saw herself at Dr. Stark's desk yesterday, saw the copper paperweight go flying, saw herself bending to pick it up, put it back where it belonged. There would be more than one set of fingerprints on that copper paperweight. One set would be *hers*.

And . . . as if that weren't bad enough, she had cut her finger on a piece of paper. It had been bleeding when she picked up that copper cube. Had she left bloodstains? They would have dried by now, but didn't the police have special tests they could conduct on an object for things like dried bloodstains? She was sure they did.

But now the paperweight was missing, anyway.

While Sid and Dinah talked around her, Shea tried to think. The office videotape would have the time and date on it. It would put her in Dr. Stark's office yesterday afternoon. It would show her stealing a copy of the exam. If the police saw that tape, they'd think Dr. Stark had found her out and confronted her. They'd think *she* had a motive for using the paperweight as a weapon. If they found the paperweight, they'd compare the fingerprints. And they'd be convinced when the prints matched that she had . . . no, they couldn't think that. They *couldn't*. The only violent act Shea Fallon had committed in her entire life was killing a housefly at summer camp.

But the police didn't know that.

She had to keep reminding herself that they didn't *have* the paperweight.

Even if they did, hers wouldn't be the only fingerprints on it. But . . . *she* was on the videotape.

Where was that tape? Did the police have it? If they did, they'd be knocking on her door any minute now.

"Let me know if you hear anything more," Shea managed before she turned and made her way down the hall on legs that felt like wet rags.

She made it. Somehow, she remained upright all the way down the hall and into her room.

Tandy wasn't there. Shea closed the door with a grateful, shaky sigh. The small, cluttered room had never seemed more welcoming. Here, she was safe. Here, she could crawl into bed and pull up the covers and shove out of her mind all thoughts of videotape and Dr. Stark and bio exams and paperweights and quarter-sized splotches of vivid red blood on the back of an unconscious skull.

It wasn't easy. She did crawl into bed, she did pull up the covers and she did fight to clear her mind. But cruel images of the fallen professor, of a bloodied paperweight, of policemen wielding handcuffs knocking at the door of Devereaux Hall's room 412 clung like barnacles until finally, nervous exhaustion banished them. Shea fell into a restless sleep.

She was awakened by the telephone's ring. She struggled upward, fighting to clear her mind. What time was it? Why was she sleeping in her clothes?

The phone shrilled insistently.

"Tandy?" Shea said groggily.

No answer. Tandy wasn't home . . .

Glancing at the clock on her bedside table, Shea saw the small hand resting on the five. Five o'clock! She'd slept the entire afternoon away.

Then she remembered. All of it. Why she had been napping in the middle of the day, something she never did. The professor . . . in the hospital . . . the exam . . . the videotape . . . the whole disastrous business washed over her, as if she were being bathed in black ink.

She groaned aloud, and reached for the phone.

"*Hello, there,*" a voice whispered.

That voice. The one from Vinnie's.

Shea sagged back against the bed pillow. Oh, no. Not this, not now.

"*I thought you might like to know what I've done for you,*" the oily whisper breathed in her ear. "*I mean, what's the point of doing something great for someone if they don't even know about it?*"

"I can't hear you very well," Shea said, finding her voice. "Who *is* this? And what are you talking about? What did you do for me?"

"*That's not important. What's important is that I did you a huge favor, and you should be grateful.*"

Shea sat up again. She strained to identify the muffled whisper, but failed. She could hardly hear it, let alone give it a face. "Tell me what you did for me," she said.

"*Say please,*" the whisper commanded coyly.

"Well, you're the one who wanted to tell me!" Shea shouted, losing her patience. "I don't care whether you tell me or not!"

"*Oh, chill out,*" the whisper admonished. "*You're not being very nice. After all, I'm sav-*"

ing you from a nasty experience. Haven't you ever seen any prison movies?"

A vision of the professor's bloodied red-brown hair flashed before Shea's eyes. "Just *tell* me," she snapped. "Or I'm hanging up."

They both knew she wouldn't do that. Not now.

"Well, pay attention then," the whisperer said, *"Because I'm only going to say this once. You never can tell who might be listening. So open your ears, Shea."*

Shea held her breath and pressed her ear so close to the receiver it felt like it was a part of her body. "I'm listening," she said then. "What did you do for me? *What?*"

The whisper wafted through the telephone line like a foul smell and, without increasing in volume, enunciated each word slowly and distinctly.

"I stole the videotape and the paperweight for you."

Chapter 5

Stunned by the revelation, Shea was unable to think straight. "What . . . what did you say?"

"You heard me. You know, you're very photogenic, Shea. Have you ever thought of a career in movies?"

Bluff, Shea's mind warned her. You can't be sure he's telling the truth. Her hand gripped the receiver so tightly, her knuckles went bone-white. "I don't know what you're talking about," she blustered.

"Oh, of course you do. I'm talking about the tape Dr. Stark had in her videocamera. The one that shows you making a copy of the exam. You must have been frantic when she said she had that film. I don't blame you. I'll bet you never dreamed when you came to Salem that you might not make it through your first year without being expelled."

True. So true. Tears of shame filled Shea's

eyes. "Are you going to give it to me?" she asked shakily. "Are you going to give me that tape?"

"Well, of course. You're its star. So you should have it."

She knew then that it wasn't going to be that easy. He wasn't going to just hand it over. He was going to make her pay.

Her voice hardened. "How much?" she demanded.

"Why, Shea, did I say one word about money?"

"How *much*?" she repeated, her eyes closed, waiting for the axe to fall, lopping off her future. What was the going rate for a future these days? And what did she do if the price was more than she could pay? Then what?

"Why don't we meet and talk about it? I hate conducting business over the phone."

Shea stared at the receiver in her hand. Meet? He wanted to talk to her in person? Then she'd know who he *was*. Didn't he care? If he had attacked Dr. Stark, what he'd done was much worse than what *she'd* done. Wasn't he afraid she'd tell?

"By the way, Shea, just in case you're interested, I wasn't stupid, like you. I didn't leave any fingerprints. The only prints on that paperweight are from your delicate little

hands. You might want to keep that in mind."

Shea sagged back against the wall. That's why he wasn't afraid to meet with her. He knew she couldn't afford to tell. The incriminating evidence only pointed to her.

He was clearly in charge here.

But . . . was it *safe* to meet with someone who would do what he was doing? Blackmail, wasn't that what it was? Who knew what he was capable of? *Someone* had attacked Dr. Stark. It was crazy to meet with him alone.

As if she had a choice.

Her tears were tears of frustration now. She'd done one stupid thing, and now she had to risk meeting with a blackmailer . . . would it ever end?

He could have made copies of the tape. If she paid him whatever he asked, he might come back later, when she thought it was all over and she was safe, and say, Gee, I forgot to mention, I just happen to have another copy . . . and another, and another, and another. . . .

Maybe it would *never* end.

Swallowing hard, she asked, "Where? Where do you want to meet?"

"I don't know yet. Haven't decided. Look for a note in your mailbox saying where and when. And," the whisper deepened, scratching like

sandpaper along the telephone line, *"be there, Shea. Or be sorry."*

The line went dead.

No, oh no . . . he was going to make her *wait*? She couldn't stand that. As much as she dreaded meeting with him, she wanted this awful business *finished*! If that was possible. . . .

How long was he going to keep her dangling?

And how long would it be before she totally and completely lost her mind?

Shea was still sitting on her bed, immobile, when Tandy arrived twenty minutes later. Shea knew it was exactly twenty minutes because she'd been staring at the clock ever since she hung up. Unable to move, she had replaced the receiver and sat there watching the minute hand slowly, steadily, circle the small, round face on her clock radio. She'd had to fight the urge to reach out and grab the thin, metal hand and stop it in its path, keep time from moving onward, toward that moment when, one way or another, she was going to have to face the music.

Ruining a perfectly good clock radio wasn't going to save her.

"What's up?" Tandy asked breathlessly, dropping her books on her bed. The first thing she did when her hands were free was what she always did, first thing, when she got up in the morning, whenever she came in from outside, and any number of times in between. She brushed her hair.

Tandy had beautiful hair. It was the color of lemonade, naturally wavy, and fell to her waist. Tandy admitted that taking care of it was a pain, but quickly added that she couldn't stand the thought of cutting it. Her swim coach nagged at her constantly to cut it, but she adamantly refused. Periodically, she had the ends trimmed at the mall beauty salon, but never allowed more than half an inch removed.

Shea might have thought then that it was a little weird. But she didn't now. Watching in envy as Tandy, standing in front of the dresser mirror, moved a brush through the thick, pale strands, she wished *she* had something to hide behind.

When she didn't answer, Tandy turned away from the mirror. "Shea? What's wrong? Are you sick? You look like you just woke up. Didn't you go to your afternoon classes?" She whirled to face the mirror again. "I hope it isn't anything catching. I can't afford to be sick these last few weeks of school."

That was Tandy, all right. Thinking mostly of Tandy. Her self-absorption was one reason they had never become really close friends, like so many other roommates had. She had insisted on the bed nearest the window. She had asked for the larger dresser, which Shea had agreed to because Tandy clearly had more clothes than she did. And if Tandy was home on evenings when Shea invited friends in, she always asked Shea to take them downstairs to the lounge, saying she needed "peace and quiet" to study. Fortunately, she dated a lot and wasn't home most evenings.

"I guess you heard about Doctor Stark," Tandy said, peering into the mirror to study her reflection more closely. What she saw seemed to satisfy her. She walked over and sat down on her bed, propping her feet up on the pile of books she'd dumped there. "Creepy, right? I know you couldn't stand her, but even you can't be happy about this."

Shea had been expecting that. Tandy didn't know the meaning of the word "tact." "That's a crummy thing to say. I think what happened to Dr. Stark is horrible. Have you heard how she is?"

Tandy opened a textbook. "Yeah," she answered, not looking up, "I heard she might be paralyzed."

Shea gasped. "Paralyzed. But . . ."

"I was in the library, and the assistant librarian said Dr. Stark can't move her legs at all."

Shea was speechless. Paralyzed? Couldn't move her legs? The thought of Dr. Stark, who strode along campus paths and sidewalks as if she owned them, never doing so again, was sickening.

"I wonder who'll take her classes?" Tandy mused aloud. "Maybe that cute T.A., the one who helps us at the computer."

Shea wasn't listening. Was the person who had rendered Dr. Stark immobile the same person who had whispered in her ear earlier? And if it was, did he know yet what the consequences of his cruel act were? Would he care?

Maybe not.

How soon would she find a note in her mailbox? Could it be there already? He might have slipped it in there as soon as they'd finished talking.

"I'm going downstairs to check my mail," she said abruptly, and got up.

Without looking up, Tandy said, "Bring mine, too, okay?"

Tandy could use a good maid. Oh, well. "Sure. Be right back."

Tandy turned on her radio and, as music filled the room, returned to her book.

She doesn't seem all that upset by what happened to Dr. Stark, Shea thought as she left the room. It was Tandy who had defended the teacher at Vinnie's when everyone else was trashing her. Yet she had passed on the news of possible paralysis so casually, as if she were talking about a hangnail.

Well, Tandy wouldn't win any awards for having great depth or compassion, Shea told herself. You already knew that.

Okay, that's true, she argued silently, but a teacher she'd said she admired might never walk again, and all Tandy Dominic can think of is whether or not someone "cute" will take Dr. Stark's place?

Depressing.

As she neared the long row of brass mailboxes recessed into the lobby wall, she put Tandy's lack of compassion out of her mind, replacing it with her own predicament. Would the note be there already?

She didn't want it to be there. Because if it wasn't, she could force the whole ugly business out of her head until morning. Maybe, if she worked really hard at it, she could even convince herself, just for today, that life was perfectly fine.

Impossible. Never happen.

Then she decided she *wanted* the note to be there. The suspense of waiting a whole night would kill her. Better to get it over with, see what he really had in mind for her.

She wanted — she didn't want — she wanted . . .

Unlocking the mailbox, she reached one hand in and let her fingers explore.

Nothing.

She was going to have to wait.

Wait . . . with her nerves on edge, her teeth clenched . . . wait for the knock on the door from the police . . . for another call from the whispered voice, wait . . .

Chapter 6

Shea waited . . . waited . . . waited. There were no more weird phone calls, no notes in her mailbox. The campus grapevine told her that Dr. Stark was recuperating slowly and that the police had no clue as to the identity of her attacker. The young teaching assistant who took over her classes was female, much to Tandy's disappointment. Shea studied and went out with Coop and her friends and had almost allowed herself to forget about the phone call, about the telltale paperweight, about that terrible afternoon in Dr. Stark's office. Almost . . .

And then one sunny, warm afternoon a few days later she unlocked her mailbox and reached inside to pull out her mail. And there it was — a sheet of white notebook paper, folded in half, ripped unevenly along one border. Her name was scrawled across the front in black ink. SHEA FALLON.

Without unfolding the piece of paper, Shea closed and locked the mailbox. Her breathing became erratic as she left the wall of boxes and slipped in through the door to the fire stairs. She didn't want to be seen reading the note.

Shea unfolded the paper, but could hardly read it because of the dim lighting. She strained to make out the letters.

The words were misspelled and scrawled in such a way that the entire note looked like the work of a first-grader.

> *Dere Shea,*
> *Mete me at midnite tonite*
> *in the woods behind Nightmare*
> *Hall. Down by the creke.*
> *Be ther or be sory.*

The note was unsigned.

Shea let the note drop into her lap and sat on the step for a long time. Here it was, at last. Hadn't she known it would show up, sooner or later? She'd gone out with Coop, she'd sat through classes, she'd eaten meals, and washed her hair and studied and read, just as if everything in her life were normal. Fool.

Because all the time, he was *there*, waiting

. . . waiting to remind her that her life wasn't normal, and wasn't going to be . . . probably for a very long time. Maybe never again.

Sitting there forever wasn't going to do any good. She got up, clutching the note in a clenched fist.

As she climbed the fire stairs to the fourth floor, she glanced at her watch. Midnight . . . she was to meet him at midnight. It was now four o'clock in the afternoon. Eight hours. How was she was going to make it through eight whole hours? Waiting . . . waiting to see what "payment" the whisperer had in store for her.

Waiting to see what would happen if she couldn't make the "payment."

Who *was* the person whispering to her on the telephone? What did he want? Why had he stolen the videotape? And why had he picked the grounds of that ugly old house on the hill as a meeting-place?

Maybe he lived there. Shea quickly listed mentally the guys she knew who lived in the gloomy old off-campus dorm. Ian Banion? Tall, good-looking, athletic. Wouldn't be him. Ian was a terrific person, as was Jessica Vogt, his girlfriend, who also lived at Nightmare Hall. And there was Milo Keith: quiet, poetic, with a sardonic sense of humor. No, it wouldn't be Milo. He was a little off-center . . . well, maybe a lot off-center, but if Milo had something to say, he wouldn't whisper it. He'd just say it, straight out, and let you do whatever you wanted with it. Jon Shea? An incorrigible flirt, who had teased her about stealing his last name. Magazine-cover-perfect Jon? She didn't think so. Jon was too wrapped up in himself. If he was going to steal a videotape, it would be one in which he starred.

The thought of meeting some whispering, threatening stranger in those deep, dark woods behind Nightmare Hall terrified her. She was never going to get through the next eight hours. Never.

There were moments when she *wanted* time to pass quickly, wanted midnight to come, get it all over with. Then there were moments when she wanted the hours to drag as if they were slogging through tar, giving her time to think, to plan, to figure things out.

What she *really* wanted, she knew, was for someone to take a giant eraser and wipe away the past few days. So that she *hadn't* gone into that office, hadn't found the exam, hadn't copied it, and Dr. Stark wasn't lying in a hospital bed, unable to walk.

Because it seemed crucial that she act as normally as possible, she did all the things she usually did.

She ate dinner, down the road from campus at Burgers Etc., with Dinah and Sid and Coop, who, she thought, kept glancing over at her as if he had a question he wanted her to answer. But he never asked it.

She prayed that no one would mention Dr. Stark. She didn't think she could deal with that. And at first, she thought her prayer had been answered. They began talking about their summer plans.

They were all, it turned out, staying on campus. Dinah had taken a lifeguard job at the Twin Falls country club, and told them that Tandy had done the same, as had her swim teammate, Linda Carlyle. All three were considering rooming together at Nightingale Hall. Dinah also mentioned that there was a party scheduled at the house the following Monday night to celebrate the end of a successful season for the swim team.

Shea had been invited and had planned to go. But that was before she'd dug herself a bottomless pit and jumped into it. Now. . . .

Shea was surprised to learn that Sid and Coop were both vying for the same summer job in the Animal Behavior Studies lab. Only one job was available, and they were both in the running. "Who decides who gets it?" she asked.

Sid's lips turned downward. "Guess. Who's the head of the A.B.S. lab?"

"Dr. Stark? But she's . . . sick."

"That's right," Dinah said emphatically. "She won't be making any major decisions for a while. Someone else will have to decide." She smiled at Sid. "Good thing, too, Sid. She wasn't your biggest fan. I was in the lab twice when she yelled at you for not keeping the charts in order."

"She's hurt, but she's not *dead*," Sid countered. "And as far as I know, she hasn't resigned any of her positions on campus. So she might still have the final say in which one of us scientific geniuses gets the plum job of the summer. It sure would look good on my record."

"Mine, too," Coop said amiably. "Any alternative plans, Frye? In case I pull this off, I mean."

Sid shrugged. "Have to go back home and fry burgers at my dad's place like I did last summer, I guess."

Coop laughed, but Dinah looked uncertain.

She wants Sid to get it, Shea thought. So they can spend the summer together. Is that why she took the lifeguard job in the first place? Because she was sure he'd get the summer job and she wanted to be near him?

"I'm staying, too," Shea volunteered. "Summer school. I'm going to take another whack at bio, see if I can do better." She was sorry the minute the words were out of her mouth. Couldn't they talk about anything but Dr. Stark? She seemed to be haunting their booth tonight.

Coop smiled at her. "No kidding? You're staying?"

Maybe not, she thought grimly. Maybe I won't even be finishing the semester, if I don't get my hands on that videotape.

She didn't eat another bite. Her food untouched, she sat studying the faces of everyone who passed their booth, wondering if there was any way you could tell by looking at a person if they made a habit of whispering into telephones.

When they left, Shea and Coop both chose to walk back to campus. Dinah trailed along behind Sid, to his car, telling Shea she'd see her later.

"You okay?" Coop asked as they waited for a gap in the highway traffic so they could cross safely to campus. "You seem a little out of it."

Oh, she *wished*. She wished she were out of it. Out of the whole disgusting mess. Her meeting with the whisperer was still long, nerve-wracking hours away. "I'm fine," she said. "Just . . . just tired, I guess. Didn't sleep much last night."

"You're not still worried about that bio exam, are you? I thought the T. A. would have handed it back by now. Since she hasn't, the chances are that it won't even be graded now. The T. A. will probably just make up an exam of her own."

Shea stared up at him. The roar of the cars whizzing by forced her to raise her voice. "Why did you mention the exam?"

He bent his head closer. "What?"

"I said, why did you mention the exam? Why did you think I'd be worried about it?" Maybe he *did* know which office she'd been coming out of that day.

He shrugged, and as a space opened up on the highway, grabbed her hand and they hurried across to the green grass of campus. "Well, something's been on your mind. You're out in left field most of the time. I thought maybe it was that exam, that's all."

And she had been trying so hard to look normal. Whatever *that* was. Hard to remember.

"So, you really going to be here all summer?" he asked as they walked along the curving cement walkway, under huge old oaks and elms.

It was dark now, the tall, old-fashioned lamps throughout campus glowing softly. It was a sweet, soft, romantic spring evening. And Coop hadn't let go of her hand.

"I *think* I'll be here," she said cautiously. The way things were going, who knew? Maybe, by summer she'd already be back home, hiding in disgrace in her bedroom, while her humiliated parents, in hushed, embarrassed voices, told anyone who came asking for her that she wasn't "feeling well."

Coop glanced down at her. "Things will be a lot quieter around here during the summer months. We'll have more time to spend together . . . if you're interested."

Was she interested? He was nice, and smart enough to be up for an important job in the A.B.S. lab and he was very, very cute.

"I'm interested," she said softly, and was rewarded for her honesty with a long, slow kiss under a flowering crab apple tree.

Coop was smiling as they began walking again.

She wondered what he would say if she said, "Coop, how would you like to explore the woods behind Nightmare Hall with me at midnight?"

The note had said to come alone. But she didn't even know *where* in the woods she was supposed to meet the whisperer. Those were thick, very dark woods. How would she ever find him in there?

That question was answered when, after Coop had walked her to her room and kissed her good night again, she opened the door to her room and her foot slid on a piece of yellow paper lying on the floor. Someone had slipped it underneath the door.

Like the first note, it had been folded once and her name was scrawled across it.

She stooped and picked it up with shaking hands.

She unfolded it and read:

> *Dere Shea,*
> *Go up the drivway at*
> *Nitemare Hall. Turn left*
> *at the grag.*

She frowned. Grag?
Oh. Garage. Turn left at the garage.

> *Thers a path. Tak the*
> *path. Down the hill.*
> *To the creke. Thers a*
> *big rock ther. You wont*
> *see me but I'll be ther.*
> *Sit on the rock and wate*

for me.
Be ther or be sory.

It too, was unsigned.

"Love letter?" Tandy's voice asked from behind Shea's shoulder.

Shea whirled guiltily, crumpling the letter in one fist. "No, I . . ." she stammered, "Just a notice about some overdue library books."

"Right." Tandy tossed her long blonde hair and grinned. *"My* face certainly turns six different shades of red when I get an overdue notice. Well, who am I to pry? Anyway, I already know who it's from. I saw you looking very cozy with Coop. He *is* cute. I went after him, but I guess he doesn't go for blondes. Did you know he gets straight A's in bio?" Tandy smiled slyly. "Maybe he could tutor you, Shea."

Ignoring the remark, Shea thought, I don't need a tutor now. What I need is a miracle.

She filled the remaining hours with as many activities as she could cram in, to keep her mind off what lay ahead. Washed her hair. Dried it. Tried to eat the popcorn Dinah and Sid brought over before they left for a late-night frat party. The few bites she managed to put in her mouth tasted like sawdust. Went with Tandy and Linda to a movie downstairs in the lounge. A comedy. She was the only person there who never once laughed.

She had to bite her tongue after the movie to keep herself from turning to Linda and saying, "Anyone at your dorm have a thing for speaking in whispers? Making weird phone calls? Writing strange, first-gradish notes?" Or, "Oh, by the way, Linda, I'm going to be out your way around midnight tonight, should I drop in and say hi?"

When Shea announced that she was going back upstairs, Linda said sweetly, "Shea, you're awfully quiet tonight. Are you feeling okay?"

An opening . . . she could so easily have said then, "No, Linda, I'm not. I'm being tortured by someone who's blackmailing me into meeting him in the woods behind your Nightmare Hall at midnight tonight. Care to help me out with this?"

But then, of course, Linda and Tandy would have said, "Well, Shea, exactly what is it that this person is blackmailing you *with*? What have you *done*, Shea?"

She answered instead, for what felt like the thousandth time, "I'm just tired, I guess. Sorry."

When she left them in the lounge, Shea felt both relief and a sense of abandonment. It was so hard pretending she was okay when she really wasn't. But she'd felt safer when she was flanked by two strong, athletic friends. Too bad they weren't coming with her that night.

When she got back to her room, she yearned to crawl under the covers and hide, maybe forever.

But if she did, she was sure the videotape and the paperweight would go straight to the police in Twin Falls or to the campus security police. Or maybe the whisperer would first show the tape in bio class on Monday morning, as Dr. Stark had threatened. He might think that was a great idea. Hilarious.

The videotape was the real problem. If it weren't for that, the police would never bother to check her fingerprints against the ones on the paperweight.

Depressed and frightened, she lay on her bed without music or a book or magazine, until it was time to leave.

Dressing in jeans, T-shirt, and lightweight windbreaker, and old sneakers in case the woods were muddy, she took a flashlight from her desk and left the room quietly.

No one was around. She could hear muted voices in several rooms, could hear faint music playing, but the hall was deserted.

She went on foot to Nightingale Hall. It

wasn't that far. And she argued with herself all the way up the highway. What she was doing was completely stupid. Movies and television shows about blackmail had always driven her nuts. She could never understand how the victims could trust a blackmailing criminal to keep his mouth shut, money or no money. The guy was a *criminal*, for pete's sake? If he had ethics, he'd be in a different line of work.

But now she understood. She was walking in *their* shoes now, those victims, and she knew, finally, how they felt. You make a very big mistake, and then all you want to do is forget it, have it forgotten. And you'll do almost anything to make that happen.

Including wandering around deep, dark woods at midnight. . . .

When she reached the driveway leading up to Nightingale Hall, she stopped.

At midnight, the house looked even more forbidding than it did in bright daylight. The downstairs was dark, the upper floors only dimly lit. The brick seemed the same color as the black night sky.

Shea fought the urge to turn and run back to the safety of campus.

Instead, she moved up the hill beside the woods, hunting for the path. She found it without any trouble.

As she pushed aside overgrown bushes and made her way between the tall, black trees whose limbs stretched toward the night sky, every muscle in her body tensed and her teeth clenched. I'm crazy, I'm crazy as a loon, she told herself angrily. I am too stupid to live.

But she kept going, stumbling along the path illuminated by her flashlight, down the hill, toward the creek. Even in the complete darkness unbroken by moonlight, she could see, in the distance, the crystal-clear, sparkling water below her.

And then she could see the boulder, the big rock mentioned in the note, perched at the edge of the creek.

Her steps faltered. This was it. The eight eternally long hours had passed, she had done what the note instructed, and now here she was, doing the dumbest thing she had ever done in her life.

There was no one at the creek. No one standing there beside the huge boulder, no one lounging on it, grinning at her, no one wading in the creek, enjoying himself while he waited for her.

She had made a big, big mistake. She shouldn't have come. She should have done what she always shrieked at all those television victims to do, "Go to the police! Confess! Tell the truth and get it over with!"

She should have gone to the dean. Or to Dr. Stark. And told the truth.

Maybe it wasn't too late. Maybe there was some way to prove that she hadn't been in that office when Dr. Stark was attacked. Some way to save herself. . . .

She heard no footsteps, no sound at all. But suddenly, without knowing how, she *knew* someone was there.

She half-turned, waving the flashlight's beam in front of her.

Nothing. There was nothing there to see. No one standing in front of her or beside her or, as she whirled in a complete circle, behind her.

But . . .

The voice, when it came, was horribly familiar, and no louder than it had been on the telephone.

"Hi, there, Shea. Have a seat on that nice, big rock. We're going to be here a while."

Chapter 7

"Where *are* you?" Shea cried, turning from side to side, her eyes straining to follow the path of her flashlight as she aimed it into the bushes and boulders along the creekbed. "Why are you hiding?"

"What you don't see can't hurt you," the voice said mockingly. *"Anyway, you don't need to see me. All you need to do is listen, and listen carefully. I have the tape that could get you expelled. And I have the paperweight that could send you to prison. I'm prepared to give them to you, but first, you must pay the price. And remember, Shea, we get what we pay for. If you don't do exactly as I say, you get nothing."*

"But I didn't . . ."

"Shut up! Just shut up and listen."

He couldn't be that far away. He had to be close by, or the whisper would have been drowned out by the wind whistling through the treetops and by the rushing waters of the creek. She played her flashlight over the surrounding area. Nothing. She saw nothing but the woods and the boulders and the underbrush and the creek.

"Sit down on that boulder behind you," the voice ordered. *"Do it now!"*

She sat, stiffly, every muscle in her body on alert. If he came up behind her, as he'd probably done with Dr. Stark, he was *not* going to take *her* by surprise. And she had the flashlight to use as a weapon. Lightweight plastic, but better than nothing.

"Here is what you're going to do," the whisper commanded. *"Tomorrow night, about this same time, you're going to go to the Animal Behavior Studies lab. The door will be unlocked. You're going to go inside to the center table, to the glass box holding the snake they call Mariah. There's a small tag on the front of the glass, with her name and species. So you'll have no excuse for making a mistake and picking up the wrong snake."*

Picking up . . . a snake? He wanted her to capture a snake from the lab? She hated snakes. Slimy, slithery reptiles made her sick. Always had. At summer camp, she had invented some very creative excuses to avoid the nature hikes, convinced that the woods were crawling with rattlers and black-snakes.

"You're crazy," she said into the darkness. Where *was* he? Talking to someone who could see her but couldn't *be* seen made her feel like a specimen under a miscroscope. He had to be watching her, waiting to see what she'd do, how she'd react.

"I'm afraid of snakes," she added. "Terrified. What do you want a snake for, anyway?"

"You didn't let me finish. That's very rude, Shea. And I don't care what you're afraid of. Doesn't make any difference. You aren't being given a choice here, remember that. You are to pick up the snake using the noose that's hanging beside the cage. The small black handle with the loop on one end. You'll lift the cover of the cage and slip the loop over Mariah's neck. Have a bag ready. The bags are lying on the shelf under the table. When you're sure the noose is around the snake's neck, tighten it just enough to pick her up. Then you'll dump her into the bag and close the top. Quickly. That's the first part of your payment."

The *first* part? Well, no point in hearing the second part. Because she was never in a million years going to be able to perform the first part. No way.

"You've got the wrong person," she said quietly. "I can't do it. I *can't!*"

"Of course you can. And you will. The snake is perfectly harmless. Well, almost. Its poison sacs have been removed. Of course, it still has fangs, so a little caution might be in order."

Her pulse, already far too rapid, skipped a beat. "Why do you want the snake?" she asked hoarsely.

"It's just a joke. A joke, that's all. No one's going to get hurt. You'll put it in the bag and then you'll take it to Lester, sixth floor, room 620. That'll be unlocked, too. You'll open the door and take Mariah out of the bag, loosen the loop around her neck, toss her into the room and close the door. That's all there is to it. Piece of cake."

Shea's jaw dropped. "You're kidding! You want me to steal a snake and throw it into somebody's room in the middle of the night? What *for?*"

"I told you, it's a joke. Harmless fun. It's not like I'm asking you to commit murder, Shea. Chill out."

"Whose room is it?"

"You don't need to know that. Not important. I suppose you can find out easily enough, but it won't make any difference. You have to do it. Or I will take your first feature role in

films straight to the administration, along with your fingerprints on copper. I'm sure you realize that they'll be immediately turned over to the Twin Falls police."

The police . . . prison . . . "How do I know you really have them?"

"If I didn't, how would I know you were on the tape? That those were your dried blood-stains on the paperweight?"

Shea sagged back against the boulder. "If I do this" . . . but of course she wasn't going to, couldn't . . . "if I do this, will you give me the tape?

"I will. I promise."

Shea laughed harshly. She'd always laughed when they got to this part in the movies. Why would anyone be dumb enough to trust a black-mailer?

Now she knew the answer. It wasn't a matter of trust. It was a matter of having no other choice.

Still, something stubborn inside her made her say, "I don't *have* to do what you say." She said it slowly, thoughtfuly, as if she were thinking out loud. "I can go straight to the administration and tell them the truth. And take my medicine."

"Maybe you could have before Dr. Stark ended up in the hospital. Maybe they wouldn't

even have expelled you. Just put you on pro-bation. But now . . . well, use your imagi-nation."

Shea swallowed, hard. As long as he was willing to give her the tape and the paper-weight, maybe she still had a chance to turn things around. She'd do what he said, then if he kept his word, she'd destroy the paper-weight and the tape when she got them. It wouldn't be like she was destroying valuable evidence. Both pieces of evidence pointed to *her*, and *she* hadn't bludgeoned Dr. Stark.

"Are you *sure* that's all I have to do . . . get the snake and take it to Lester? Then you'll give me the tape?"

"I will," the voice repeated. *"Honor among thieves and all that. Do as I tell you, and the tape is yours."*

There was a slight rustling sound in the woods behind her, then silence.

"Are you still here?" Shea asked uncertainly. "Where will I meet you so you can give me the tape?"

No answer.

He was gone.

She had her orders. Now, all she had to do was decide whether or not she could carry out the task assigned. And if she decided she couldn't, she'd have to come up with a way out.

Any way you sliced it, she was in for twenty-four hours of agonizing, of not eating, not sleeping, no peace, no quiet, no safety, her nerves shrieking.

Shea stood, glancing through the woods and up the hill toward faint lights shining from Nightmare Hall's windows. It seemed so ironic, so unfair, that Tandy, sleeping in that creepy old house, was far safer, after all, than Shea was.

Chapter 8

The girl sitting behind the reception desk at Lester looked up without interest when Shea entered the deserted, tile-floored lobby the next morning. "Up early, aren't you?" she said irritably. Her nap had been interrupted.

"Who's in room 620?" Shea asked abruptly.

Without checking, the girl answered, "Bethany Briggs and Annette Driscoll." Then she closed her eyes again.

As Shea headed back to her own dorm, she thought about the two girls. Shea knew both girls, although not well. Bethany was a pale, quiet girl with straight blonde hair, who never spoke up in class. Annette was just the opposite: tall, gorgeous, very outgoing, and popular. Some people called the roommates "The Odd Couple" because they were so very different. And yet they seemed to be good friends.

Which of them, Shea wondered as she turned to leave, was the target of tonight's practical joke? Would one of them really find the snake stunt funny?

Or . . . had one of the roommates somehow made the whisperer angry? Was this his way of getting revenge?

Shea shook her head. Thinking that way was dangerous. Because if she believed it was anything more than a simple, harmless practical joke, she'd never be able to go through with it. It was going to be close to impossible as it was.

"Whatever you're thinking about, it must be heavy stuff," an amused voice said from behind her as she reached out to pull Devereaux's wooden door open.

Coop. Standing before her as she turned around. He was smiling, as if he was glad to see her. "How about breakfast?" he suggested. "Maybe food will snap you back to reality. Not in the dining hall, though. Mrs. Doyle didn't raise stupid children. Feel like hiking up the road to Burgers Etc.? They make a mean omelet."

She hadn't planned to eat. Now that she knew who was in room 620, she had planned to do nothing on this beautiful spring day but hide in her bed, talking to no one, trying to gear up for what she had to do at midnight.

But . . . shouldn't she be acting normal? If she hid out all day, there would be questions from her friends. "What's wrong, Shea?" "Are you sick, Shea?" She could hardly say, "Well, it's like this, I need all my energy for this disgusting thing I have to do tonight if I don't want to end up in prison."

"Breakfast sounds great," she said, hoping Coop wouldn't pick up on how phony that sounded. How sensitive was he, anyway?

Sensitive enough, she learned a short while later to notice that she wasn't eating anything.

"You okay?" he asked, looking at her intently.

Leave me alone, she wanted to say. Don't get mixed up with me. You think I'm something I'm not. Everyone does. The truth is, I'm in a whole lot of trouble and I don't want to see the look on your face when you find out what a mess I've made of things.

She didn't say any of that. All she said was, "I thought I was hungry, but I'm not." And then she surprised herself by bringing up a subject she had thought she didn't want to discuss. The words just slipped out of her mouth before she could stop them. "Have you heard any more about Dr. Stark?"

Coop shook his head, sending a strand of

dark hair sliding across his forehead. He pushed it back impatiently. "She still can't walk. That's all I know. Haven't heard anything about the summer job in the lab yet, either."

"Dinah said Dr. Stark wasn't wild about Sid," Shea said. "Isn't that a good sign? For you, I mean?"

Coop laughed. "She yelled at everyone in the lab, not just Sid. And she came up behind me in the hall one day and heard me telling Tandy I wondered where Stark parked her broomstick."

Coop's expression turned grim. "My whole life flashed before my eyes when I saw her standing there. I could feel that summer job slipping right out of my hands and into Sid's. But . . . that was before she ended up in the hospital. Now, who knows? Maybe someone who doesn't hate my guts will make the decision."

Shea almost asked Coop then about the snake named Mariah. He'd know whether or not the snake really was harmless. Or she could always ask Sid. Even Dinah, who often stopped in the lab to visit Sid and talk to the animals.

But she couldn't ask any of them about it. Because if she did, who was the first person they'd suspect when the snake turned up missing? Their good friend, Shea Fallon.

Burgers Etc. was packed with sleepy people sipping coffee, wolfing down pancakes, talking about weekend plans. Shea's eyes scanned the long, narrow diner, wondering again what kind of face she should attach to the sinister, whispering voice. Was it a tall voice, a short voice, was it thin or fat, blonde or brunette, male or female. . . . ?

The last thought startled her. She'd been thinking of the deep whisper as male. But of course it could be female. How could you tell from a whisper?

"Feel like taking in a movie tonight?" Coop asked casually as they got up to leave.

Oh, gee, I'd love to, she answered silently, but I've got a snake to steal. Aloud, she said, "Can't, sorry. I have to . . . study."

"Tomorrow's Sunday," he pointed out. "No classes."

"That doesn't mean I don't have to study," she said sharply. Why couldn't he just take no for an answer? Hadn't anyone ever told him no? "I'm really behind," she added in a milder tone. It wasn't *his* fault she was such a wreck. "I need every spare moment I can find, or I'm not going to make it through finals."

"Dinah will be disappointed." He held the heavy glass door open for her and they left the diner. "She and Sid are going, too. I told her I'd try to talk you into making it a foursome."

Sid and Dinah? Sid and Dinah almost never doubled. Sid didn't like "sharing" his time with Dinah. At least, that's what Dinah always said.

"Dinah will understand," Shea said. "She gets straight A's without blinking an eye, but she knows I don't."

"She wasn't getting an A in bio," Coop said, taking Shea's hand to lead her across the highway.

Shea looked up at him in surprise. "She wasn't? How do you know?"

"Sid told me. He said Dinah was really shook. Apparently, she'd argued with Dr. Stark about two of her grades this semester, thought they were unfair. But Stark refused to budge."

Frowning, Shea said, "She never told me that."

"Tell you the truth," Coop went on, "I think Dinah's a little bit relieved that Stark won't be finishing out the year. Probably thinks she'll have a better chance with someone else. Dinah would never say that, of course. She's too nice."

No, she's not, Shea thought, remembering the night at Vinnie's when they'd all been raking Dr. Stark over the coals. Dinah had been as vocal as anyone in her criticism of the teacher. Shea hadn't thought anything of it then, because they were all doing it. Now, she realized that it *had* been unlike Dinah to be so critical. She must have been really upset about her grade in Dr. Stark's class.

But then, why not? Hadn't they all been? Tandy was the only one who'd defended Dr. Stark.

"Let me know if you change your mind about the movie," Coop said as he left Shea on the steps of the campus library. "I'll be at the lab all morning. You can call me there."

At the mention of the lab, her face must have paled, because he quickly added, "Shea? What's wrong?"

"Headache," she said quickly. "See you." She turned to run up the steps and inside the dim, cool library, where she could sit and think in privacy.

She stayed in the library for a while, until she began to feel as if she were suffocating. Then she went out and hiked along the river behind campus. It amazed her that people passing by called out to her, wanted to stop and talk, asked her about her weekend plans. As if she were still the same, normal, popular person she'd been when the week began. Couldn't they *see* that she wasn't?

Later that day she played tennis with Tandy,

who finally became so exasperated with Shea's sloppy, erratic playing that she threw down her racket in despair.

While playing, Shea remembered how often they'd seen Dr. Stark on the courts. Although the teacher had exchanged the dowdy print dresses for tennis whites, her hair was still severely pulled back from her face, her mouth set in a grim, straight line as she fought to win. She had never looked to Shea as if she were having any fun at all.

Shea couldn't help thinking then that Dr. Stark might never play tennis again. The thought had depressed her so profoundly, she'd missed a perfect serve from Tandy, who had groaned and given her a disgusted look.

Later, she had dinner with Tandy and Linda Carlyle at Hunan Manor in town, but turned down their invitation to attend a sorority party with them. Then she went back to her room to lie on her bed and watch the hands on her clock radio approaching the time when she would have to leave for the lab.

Suddenly she found herself standing outside the door to the Animal Behavior Studies lab, her hand on the round brass knob.

The hallway was dark and deserted, the building quiet. The teachers and teaching assistants and laboratory technicians and student volunteers, like Coop and Sid, were, at the witching hour on a spring night, partying or watching television or seeing a movie or listening to music or reading or, maybe, sleeping. The reptiles and the spiders and the mice and the rats were, like her, on their own.

There was no sound from inside the lab.

Shea turned the knob and the door, unlocked as the whisperer had promised, opened.

When she had closed the door behind her, she switched on her small plastic flashlight. She had never been in the lab before. Forcing herself to take a few slow deep breaths, she glanced around, using the flashlight to study the room.

There were the mice, in their cages on tables to her right, the larger rats in cages beside them.

She moved hesitantly into the room until she was standing beside a long, narrow table with a bottom shelf. She saw the bags on the shelf before she could work up the courage to study the table's contents.

Cages. Two, three, four.

Glass, like aquariums. With covers, also glass.

Shea closed her eyes. She couldn't look.

How was she going to carry out her "assignment"?

You have to do this, she told herself. You have no choice. So just *do* it and get it over with!

Shea opened her eyes. Nothing stirred in any of the cages. She was grateful for that much. A sleeping snake was preferable to an alert, slithering one, its narrow, forked little tongue spitting at her in defiance.

She located the cage housing the snake named Mariah. All coiled up like a spring in a corner of its cage. She drew in her breath when she spied the rattle at one end, but quickly reminded herself that the snake had been rendered harmless.

"Harmless, harmless, harmless," she whispered, as if chanting the word repeatedly could somehow protect her. But a niggling little voice in the back of her mind said, "He said it wasn't poisonous anymore, but it can still *bite*."

Shea forced herself to study the cage's lid. A simple slice of glass, hooked firmly on two sides. With her eyes on the snake, she undid the hooks with trembling fingers. But she didn't lift the lid. Not yet.

Keeping her eyes on the sleeping Mariah, she reached down with one hand to grasp one of the bags from the bottom shelf. It was a gunny sack made of beige canvas, with a drawstring closure. She dropped the sack onto the table beside the cage and yanked its neck fully open.

The stick with the noose on one end was right where the whisperer had said it would be, hanging on the left side of the glass cage. Shea reached for it tentatively, willing her hand not to shake.

I am actually going to *do* this, she thought with a mixture of horror and awe. I'm going to pick up this tool . . . and she did. I'm going to lift the lid of this cage . . . and she did. I'm going to reach in and loop the noose around this snake's head and then I'm going to tighten the noose and then I'm going to pick the snake up and drop it into that sack and carry it out of here.

This she did not do. Because the snake was asleep, its head cozily resting inside that coil of reptile flesh. There was no way she could get the noose around its head while it was asleep.

She would have to wake it up.

Shea tapped lightly on the glass, then more firmly.

The noise woke up the snake.

It lifted its head sleepily, fastening cold, beady eyes on Shea.

Afraid the snake would lie back down and the moment of opportunity would be lost, Shea moved quickly, automatically. She dropped the loop into place, the noose sliding easily over the snake's head, and jerked the stick backward so the loop tightened gently.

She had done it. Her knees were so weak she had to lean against the table, and her breath was coming in painful, choked little gasps, but she had done what she had thought she could never do.

Swiftly, before her shaking fingers could accidentally let go of the stick, dropping it back into the cage, Shea lifted the startled reptile and thrust it into the waiting sack. With her free hand, she yanked on the drawstring, pulling the neck of the sack tightly closed, with half of the stick protruding from the top so that she would be able to grab it when it was time to unleash the snake on room 620.

Done!

The snake was hers.

Her knees were knocking against each other, her arms felt like all of her bones had melted and her lower lip was quivering uncontrollably, but . . . she had done it.

Except . . .

Except that she wasn't finished.

Chapter 9

As she hurried from the lab across a deeply shadowed campus to Lester, Shea held the canvas bag away from her, as if it were a ticking time bomb. She could feel the writhing movements of the shocked and protesting Mariah, angry at being yanked out of a contented sleep.

Campus was deserted. Those who weren't out partying were in their rooms studying or sleeping. Shea was grateful. What could she possibly say to someone who caught her running across campus holding a wriggling gunnysack out in front of her as if it were about to explode?

She darted into Lester, and, unwilling to risk encountering someone in the elevator, took the stairs to the sixth floor. Her heart was pounding ferociously and, by the time she reached the fourth floor landing, she felt dizzy and lightheaded.

But she kept going, telling herself it would all be over soon. In just a few more minutes, she'd pull off this stupid stunt and retreat to her own room. Tomorrow, she'd get the tape and the paperweight, destroy them, and put all of this nastiness behind her and get on with her life.

Room 620 was quiet, with no light shining under the door. Bethany and Annette were either asleep or out.

A door slammed somewhere.

Shea jumped and almost dropped the noose handle. The possibility that she might actually have to reach into the bag and fumble around for the handle made her blood freeze. She pulled the door open quietly, carefully. As she did, her other hand jerked the handle and the snake free and, in one frantic movement, tossed snake *and* noose into the room. Then she turned to leave. But in her haste, she pulled the door closed with too much force.

It slammed.

Behind it, she heard. "What? What was that?" and then a second voice ordering, "Turn on the light, quick!"

Shea ran, the canvas bag dangling from her wrist.

Half a second later, a scream shattered the midnight quiet. It was quickly followed by another, and another until the sixth floor resounded with screams.

Shea stopped running. She wasn't going to make it down the entire length of the hallway unseen. Doors were going to fly open. Heads were going to appear in the open doorways. What those curious eyes would see was a hallway occupied by only one person. Her. With a canvas bag clearly labeled PROPERTY OF A.B.S. LAB hanging from her wrist.

When, minutes later, they learned that the reason for the screaming was a reptile from the A.B.S. lab, anyone with an IQ above twelve would make the connection.

She had to get rid of the sack.

Her eyes darted wildly about, seeking a trash bin, a closet, anything . . .

There, in the wall opposite her . . . an incinerator chute.

The telltale bag disappeared only seconds before heads began appearing in doorways.

The screaming continued, reaching an hysterical pitch. People began moving out of their rooms, asking each other what was going on, some complaining about the nerve-shattering sound. Somebody shouted, "Hey, who's partying and why wasn't I invited?"

Shea slipped into the gathering pack making its way toward room 620. She had to know what was going on in there. It didn't sound at all as if the "joke" had been funny.

More doors flew open, more bare feet joined the group hurrying along the hallway toward 620. Several people, including Shea, broke into a run as it became clear that the screaming was in earnest. There was no party going on in that room. Something was very, very wrong.

They were just a few feet away when the door suddenly flew open and a wild-eyed Annette appeared in the doorway. Her dark hair hung in a tangled heap on her shoulders and her pretty face was ashen. "Help me!" she screamed, "someone, *help*! I think Bethany's had a heart attack. Hurry!"

Shea froze. Heart attack? Bethany?

"And someone come and get this . . . this repulsive *creature* out of here?" Annette screamed from inside the room.

Bethany was only eighteen. How could she have had a heart attack?

A boy from Shea's English class ran into the room, emerging a moment later holding Mariah aloft by the noose handle. There were cries of revulsion from the crowd.

"That's from the lab," someone called. "What was it doing in their room?"

"Scaring them half to death," the snakehandler replied grimly. "Bethany's out cold. Annette already called campus emergency." He shook his head.

Shea moved to the open doorway and stared inside, where several girls were helping Annette in her efforts to revive Bethany. The stricken girl lay prone on the floor, arms outstretched. Her lips were tinged with blue.

"She's always been so careful," Annette was saying as she dabbed at her roommate's forehead with a damp cloth. "Didn't go out for sports, even though she wanted to, hardly ever went dancing . . . I always felt bad because I go dancing a lot and she couldn't come along. She's careful about what she eats, and she'd been feeling really good lately. And now this! I can't believe it! Why would someone throw a snake into the room of someone with a heart condition?"

Shea sagged backward, against the door. Heart condition? Bethany had a heart condition? Had the whisperer known that?

Of course he had.

And that changed everything. Tossing a snake inside room 620 had never been intended as a prank. Couldn't have been. She had been blackmailed into doing something that could have taken someone's *life*.

"Boy, you look worse than Bethany," a girl standing next to Shea said to her. "Maybe you should leave. This whole scene too much for you?"

Yes, it was. That poor girl lying on the floor, corpselike, while out in the hall the snake was still on display. Yes, it was all too much for Shea. At any moment, she just might start screaming herself.

But she couldn't leave. Not yet. Not until she learned that Bethany was going to be all right . . . *if* Bethany was going to be all right.

After what seemed like hours, the paramedics arrived.

"She's just fainted," one paramedic announced when she had performed a cursory examination of the patient.

Shea let out a huge sigh of relief. Annette, kneeling beside Bethany, did the same.

"But she could be experiencing some minor cardiac distress," the woman continued. "We're going to take her with us, check her out thoroughly." She glanced at Annette. "You said something scared her?"

"Yes. A snake. Someone tossed it into our room. Bethany is deathly afraid of snakes. She got hysterical the minute she saw what it was. And then she collapsed."

Shea heard "deathly afraid of snakes" and felt a surge of pure hatred toward the whispering voice on the telephone. A "joke," he had said. "Perfectly harmless," he'd told her.

Bethany could have *died*.

Annette went with the ambulance, Mariah was taken back to the lab, and the crowd began to disperse. Shea headed wearily back to Devereaux.

The phone was ringing when Shea quietly unlocked the door and entered her room.

She stared through the dark toward the ringing telephone. No . . . no, it couldn't be, not *now*!

"Mmm, get that, will you?" Tandy murmured sleepily, and buried her head under her pillow.

Moving stiffly, like a puppet, Shea walked over and picked up the receiver with an icy hand.

"*Congratulations*," came the sinister whisper. "*You done good, kiddo! Real good!*"

Chapter 10

Shea was not about to talk to the whisperer with Tandy in the room. Without saying a word, she slammed the receiver down and unplugged the phone. It wasn't as if anyone else would be calling them this late.

"Who *was* that?" Tandy muttered, emerging from beneath her pillow.

"Wrong number." Shea said irritably, as she got into bed.

A joke . . . it was supposed to be a joke. Now Bethany was in the infirmary . . . and the whisperer still had the videotape and the paperweight. It was all supposed to be over by now, and it wasn't.

She rolled over on her back again and wondered if it ever would be over.

She shouldn't have slammed the phone down like that. Maybe he'd called to tell her he was ready to keep his promise.

What if she'd made him so angry, he'd decided not to keep his promise at all?

And did it really matter, Shea thought wearily as the sleep of total exhaustion overtook her, after what had happened to Bethany?

The following morning, she half-expected the telephone to ring immediately when she plugged it in. It didn't. But as long as she was in the same room with it, she couldn't relax.

"I'm going over to the infirmary to check on Bethany," she told Tandy. She had already filled Tandy in on the snake episode, carefully omitting her part in it.

"Are you going to stop in and say hello to Dr. Stark while you're there?" Tandy asked with a teasing grin. "I know how much you must miss her."

"Dr. Stark? She's at the hospital in town."

"They're supposed to transfer her up here this morning." Tandy began brushing the long, pale yellow waves. "Coop told me. I'm surprised he didn't tell you. Dr. Stark wanted to be back on campus. They thought she'd get better faster if she was around her beloved students." Tandy's tone was heavy with sarcasm. "Because you all love her so much, I guess."

"Tandy . . ."

"So they transferred her to the infirmary to

recuperate. I'm sure the line of visitors will go all the way around the building." More sarcasm. "She still can't walk, so a physical therapist comes out from Twin Falls every day to work with her." Tandy laughed. "Now, there's a job for you. I think Stark is a great teacher, but I wouldn't want to be the person who has to force her to do painful exercises. One withering glance, and the poor therapist will probably run for the hills."

Shea wondered briefly when Tandy had talked to Coop. She wasn't still interested in him, was she?

Shea walked to the window and looked out over campus. A quiet Sunday morning, the slate-gray sky promising rain before noon. Good. Gloomy weather would match her mood. The sun had no business shining when so many things were wrong.

"Want to come with me?" she asked as she turned away from the window.

"Can't. Heavy date. I'm going canoeing with Paul Sanderson from psych class."

Paul, not Coop. Good. "I don't think so, Tandy." Shea slipped into a pair of jeans and khaki crop top. "It's going to pour. Your canoe will get swamped."

Tandy shrugged. "Then we'll do something else. I hardly know Bethany, Shea. If you want to play angel of mercy, be my guest, but count me out."

"I thought you were one of Dr. Stark's few fans. Aren't you going to visit her?"

"I can't stand being around sick people. Besides, would I really cancel a great date to spend time with a bio teacher? Reality check, Shea."

Shea went to the infirmary alone.

Bethany was awake, but she was still ghostly white, with navy-blue shadows under her eyes. She lay quietly in the infirmary bed. She seemed surprised to see Shea. Annette, sitting in a straight-backed wooden chair beside the patient's bed, looked equally surprised.

I don't blame them, Shea thought, wondering if she'd made a grave tactical error. She didn't know Bethany very well, either. Wasn't her unexpected visit likely to arouse suspicion?

She felt as if the word GUILTY was emblazoned across her face in vivid red paint. "I . . . I was visiting Dr. Stark," she said hastily. "Thought I'd just stop in and see how you were doing, Bethany. Are you okay?" Say yes, Shea commanded silently.

"Sure," Bethany answered quietly. "I'm fine, Shea. It was nice of you to stop by. Have you heard if they've found out who threw that horrible thing into our room?"

Conscious of Annette's brown eyes on her, Shea somehow managed to say, "No, I haven't. But I'm sure it was just meant as a stupid practical joke."

"Some joke!" Annette said with contempt.

Shea couldn't stay another second. If she did, she was liable to confess everything and beg Bethany and Annette to forgive her.

"Glad you're feeling better," she said. "Gotta go. I'm going to spend this lovely rainy day hitting the books."

"If you hear anything," Annette said, "about who did this, I mean, let us know."

Shea thought for a split second that she saw something in Annette's eyes, heard something in her voice.

I *don't* know anything about the person behind it, she thought as she approached the reception desk. Except that he whispers. And enjoys making people dance to his tune. That's all I know.

Afraid that Annette or Bethany might find out that she hadn't been there to visit Dr. Stark, Shea impulsively asked the receptionist, "Is Dr. Stark seeing visitors?"

The receptionist, who appeared to be a student volunteer, laughed. "If she *had* any, she'd probably see them. I don't expect a mad rush now that she's here with us. She's not exactly the most popular person on campus."

"Doesn't she have any family? Friends?"

"I guess not. The only person who's been in to see her since she got here this morning was one of her students. Guy named Cooper. He was here this morning. But he actually came to see Bethany, like you. I guess he stopped in to see Stark on the spur of the moment. Probably felt sorry for her." The receptionist regarded Shea from behind wire-rim glasses. "You want to see her? She's not in a very good mood. But what else is new?"

Shea hesitated. What were the chances that she could talk to Dr. Stark without arousing the professor's suspicion? She wasn't even sure the teacher knew her name. The class was too big. She'd think it was really weird that a student she hardly knew had come to visit.

The chances of pulling off a conversation with Dr. Stark now without revealing anything, were nil.

Still. . . .

"Where is she?" Shea asked.

The receptionist pointed to a room off to one side. The door stood open.

Shea went over and looked inside, careful to make no noise.

Dr. Stark was lying flat on her back in a long,

narrow bed draped in white. She was staring at the ceiling, a blank expression on her face.

There were no flowers, no boxes of candy, no magazines.

"Pathetic, isn't it?" A short, round nurse with curly hair appeared at Shea's side. She sighed. "I'm going to try to get her into the whirlpool. The dean had it put in for her husband. He's arthritic. Comes here every day. It should help Dr. Stark, too. Keep those muscles from atrophying."

"Isn't she getting physical therapy?"

"Not right now. She kept throwing the physical therapist out of her room at the hospital. Says he's a sadist. He was only trying to help."

Shea left the infirmary more depressed than when she arrived. She hadn't imagined that was possible.

Although it was Sunday, which meant no mail delivery, Shea checked her mailbox when she got back to Devereaux. The whisperer might have sent instructions on where and when she could pick up the tape.

The mailbox was empty.

Dinah, in shorts and a yellow tank top, got off the elevator as Shea turned away from the mailbox.

"Where are you off to?" Shea asked.

"To the A.B.S. lab. Sid wants me to meet him there. Want to come? Coop might be there, too."

"Dinah, you know what Sid always says. Three's a crowd. Or four, or five, or any more than two, as far as he's concerned."

Dinah flushed guiltily. "You're right. I'm sorry, Shea." She turned away, shoulders slumped, and pushed the door open.

"You should have an umbrella," Shea called. But Dinah had already disappeared from sight.

Sid wouldn't be happy until Dinah had no friends left at all, Shea thought as she turned and headed for her room. No one to get in his way.

When she opened the door to her room, she almost tripped over the package lying just inside. A small box, wrapped in brown paper.

Shea bent to pick it up.

And saw her name printed on the top of the package in small black letters.

Something about the handwriting set off a warning bell in Shea's head. It looked familiar. Like . . . like the note in her mailbox.

The package was from the whisperer.

Shea walked over to the bed and sat down, holding the package as if it might bite her.

She was afraid to open it. He had to be angry that she'd hung up on him last night. What if there was another snake in there?

But she had to open it. It *could* be the tape. He *had* promised. If she did what he asked . . . and she had. It *could* be in her hands right now.

Shea tore open the package. Suddenly, there it was, lying in her hands, in its black plastic case. The film that could have ruined her life. He had kept his promise. No copper paperweight in the package, but the tape was more important. The paperweight wasn't incriminating all by itself, not without her image on the videotape.

She had to view it, see just what was on it. Make sure it really was *the* tape.

Would the lounge be empty on a gloomy Sunday afternoon? Rain slapped against the windows, and tap-tapped on the roof. There would be no tennis, no canoeing, no hiking, or jogging on campus. Which could mean a crowded lounge, filled with people watching a movie on the VCR.

But she *had* to check out the tape.

Slipping the black case into her shoulder bag, she left the room and took the elevator down to the basement.

The lounge was empty.

Lunchtime. She'd forgotten it was that time of day. The dining halls and cafes at Salem

University were probably packed, but the lounge was deserted.

The large-screen television set and the VCR were housed in a tall, wide shelving unit that ran half the length of one wall. The lower half of the unit was completely enclosed, large enough for storing lots of equipment and shielded by thick wooden doors with brass handles.

Knowing that she might have very little time, Shea thrust the tape into the machine and turned it on.

She backed away, her eyes riveted to the television screen.

The first sign that something was wrong was a burst of bright, lively music. Shea took a few more steps backward, never taking her eyes off the screen.

A cat . . . chasing a mouse . . . in vivid color . . .

Shea stared with disbelieving eyes.

No. He couldn't *do* this to her. She had thought it was over, that she was safe now, that the tape she needed to stay in school, maybe even out of jail, was in her possession at last.

But what she was watching was not a videotape of a professor's office.

It was a Tom and Jerry cartoon.

Chapter 11

How could he *do* this to her?

She had done what he'd told her. She hadn't wanted to, and it had turned out even worse than she'd expected, but she *had* done it.

But he hadn't kept his promise.

And you really thought he would?

Shea slid the cassette free and turned off the VCR.

"You should never hang up on me."

The whisper caught Shea off guard. There was no one else in the lounge.

"It makes me mad," the voice continued. *"It's really very rude."*

The whispered words seemed to be coming from directly in front of her. From . . . the cabinet?

Shea bent at the waist, reached out and

tugged on the brass door handles directly beneath the TV shelf. The doors remained firmly in place.

He *had* to be in there. There was no other place.

He had guessed that she would come directly to the lounge to watch the tape. And he'd been waiting for her.

"You broke your promise!" she hissed. "I *did* what you said. It was stupid and cruel, but I *did* it. Now Bethany's in the hospital. She could have died. And I still don't have that videotape."

"You would have it if you hadn't exhibited such atrocious manners last night."

"Tandy was in the room!" Shea cried. "I couldn't talk."

"No excuses, please. Actually, it's Tandy I wish to discuss with you."

"What?" Shea stared at the cabinet. "I don't want to discuss *anything* with you. I just want that tape!"

"Sorry. Not just yet. You blew your chance when you had it. Now you're going to have to prove to me all over again how much you want it."

Furious, Shea grabbed the door handles on the cabinet again and yanked with all her might. In vain. They didn't give an inch.

"Do you know the story of Samson and De-lilah, Shea?"

"Yes!" she snapped, glancing over her shoulder to make sure the room was still empty. It was. How long before someone came in and saw her talking to the TV cabinet . . . "Delilah chopped off all of Samson's hair and robbed him of his strength. What does that have to do with anything?"

"Well, I'll tell you," the whisperer answered slyly. *"It's that roommate of yours. Tandy is so vain. Disgustingly so. Always tossing around that hair of hers."*

"She's not that bad," Shea said loyally, even as an image of Tandy combing and brushing and blow-drying and braiding and tossing the waist-long hair danced before her eyes.

Ignoring her, the whisperer continued. *"You're going to teach Tandy a lesson in hu-mility. You're going to play Delilah to her Samson."*

Voices sounded faintly in the distance. Were they approaching the lounge? "What are you talking about?" Shea asked quickly.

The whisper became harsh, with an edge to it. *"By tomorrow morning, Tandy had better have only a few inches of hair left on her head, or that videotape will be in the hands of the police by noon."*

Shea gasped. "You want me to cut off her hair? Why? That's crazy!"

"Don't you dare call me crazy! I told you, she needs to be taught a lesson. She needs to learn that beauty is only skin-deep." A wicked laugh, then, *"Or should I say hair-follicle deep? Just do it, Shea."*

The voices were coming closer. And they were definitely headed for the lounge. "I won't! I am not doing something so stupid and cruel. Do whatever you want with the tape and the paperweight. I'm not touching one hair on Tandy's head."

"Someone's coming. Turn around, now, and leave this room. Don't look back or you'll be sorry. And Shea, if Tandy shows up on campus tomorrow with long hair, your college days are over. And you'll be wearing prison stripes instead of a university sweatshirt. Now go!"

Shea turned and hurried out of the room, arms hugging her chest to keep herself from turning around.

But when she reached the wide archway, she slipped around the corner into the hall and stayed there. She couldn't leave yet. If there was even the slightest chance that she might catch a glimpse of the creep who was making her life so miserable, she couldn't pass it up.

But the whisperer mustn't see her peeking.

Slowly, carefully, she peered around the edge of the doorframe.

Just in time to see a pair of shoes disappear behind a side door.

She had waited too long to look.

Furious with herself, she concentrated on the tiny glimpse. Black shoes? Brown? Low-heeled. Blood red laces . . . one of the school's colors. Lots of people wore them. Were those a man's shoes? A woman's?

She couldn't be sure.

Angry and disappointed, Shea sagged against the wall. The whisperer wanted her to cut off Tandy's hair? Crazy. Insane. She wasn't going to do it, of course.

"Hey, Shea, what've you got there?" Tom Neilsen said as he and a group of friends arrived at the entrance to the lounge. He was pointing at the cassette in her left hand. "Anything good?"

She looked down at the tape. She'd forgotten all about it. "Here," she said, extending it toward Tom, "you can have it. It's a Tom and Jerry cartoon. Have a good laugh on me."

Tom took the tape. "Thanks! Want me to drop it back at your room later?" He looked hopeful.

Shea shook her head. "Just keep it. It's not what I thought I was getting." Waving, she turned and left.

Coop was waiting in the hall outside her room when she arrived. His dark hair was damp from walking in the rain. "Feel like seeing a movie?" he asked when she said hello. "Seems like the perfect day to be inside and I haven't seen any of the movies at the mall. Have you?"

Shea shook her own damp head. "No. But I thought you guys all went last night. You and Sid and Dinah."

"That fell through." Coop slipped out of his blood red Salem U. windbreaker and shook the excess rainwater from it before putting it back on. "I guess Sid decided he'd rather have Dinah all to himself. Called me and said they'd changed their minds."

"They didn't go, either?"

Coop shrugged. "I guess not. So, you up for it?"

Going to a movie was definitely better than sitting in her room fixating on what had just happened in the lounge. There wasn't a single thing she could do about her jeopardized college career on a Sunday afternoon. All of the offices were closed. If she was going to go to the dean and confess, it would have to wait until Monday.

"Sure. Why not?" she said as she opened the door.

"Your enthusiasm is underwhelming," Coop said, a slight edge to his voice. "If there's something else you'd rather do, just say so."

She looked up at him in surprise.

He flushed. "Sorry. This stupid competition thing for the A.B.S. lab job is getting to me. No one seems to be able to tell us when the word might come down. I need to know if I have to make other plans."

"I'm sure you won't," she said staunchly, although she really had no idea which way the decision would go. She supposed that depended on who made it: Dr. Stark, or someone else.

Maybe she wouldn't go to the dean. Maybe she'd go straight to Dr. Stark. Why not? What was the worst thing an invalid in a hospital bed could do to her?

Whatever happened, it would be a huge relief to get it off her chest, off her mind.

Making the decision to confess freed Shea's mind to enjoy the movie, a comedy. She had forgotten how great it felt to laugh. The huge lump that she'd been carrying around in her chest began to dissolve.

I should have told the truth right away, she thought as they left the theater. Whatever had happened then couldn't have been much worse than what the whisperer has done.

Cut Tandy's beautiful hair? Never!

Shea was surprised to find Tandy and Paul, Sid and Dinah clustered together under the mall's marquee, away from the rain, when Shea and Coop emerged. Sid didn't look very pleased.

Oh, lighten up! Shea thought with disgust, you're Dinah's boyfriend, not her *warden*. She has a right to be with her friends.

Although Sid seemed reluctant when Coop suggested they all go to Vinnie's, Dinah pleaded and Sid gave in. But he didn't look happy about it.

The restaurant was crowded, the jukebox music loud, the smells of garlic and tomato sauce welcoming when they arrived.

"See?" Dinah said to Sid in a placating voice as they all slid into one of the larger booths. "Isn't this a great place to be on a gloomy, rainy night?"

"Sure," Sid responded crankily, "if you like being crammed into a booth like sardines in a can."

Everyone ignored hm.

When they had ordered, Sid, Coop, and Paul

went off to play pool and Tandy headed for the restroom.

"Her hair," Dinah said knowingly, a broad grin on her face. "Hasn't touched it in at least five minutes. Probably suffering withdrawal pangs."

The mention of Tandy's hair made Shea's stomach feel queasy. "I thought you and Sid were meeting at the A.B.S. lab," she said, to change the subject. "How did you end up at the mall?"

"The door was locked. Sid couldn't believe it. They never locked it before. But I guess they're not taking any chances any more."

"Doesn't Sid have a key?"

"If he did, he's lost it. And he can't very well get another one from Dr. Stark now. He'll have to wait until he finds out who's replacing her. Then I guess he'll get one. Anyway, we decided to see a movie instead."

"I'm glad you did." Shea meant it. "I've hardly seen you all week." Not that she hadn't been preoccupied with problems of her own. Still . . . "Sid really doesn't believe in sharing, does he? I can't believe you put up with that."

Dinah flushed. "Oh, Shea, don't start. You just don't understand. Besides, you haven't exactly been beating a path to my door. I've called you a couple of times, and there wasn't any answer." She smiled. "I guess Coop's been keeping you busy."

Shea, tired of keeping her terrible burden to herself, might have spilled the whole story then, but the others returned and the moment was lost.

They were halfway through their meal when Milo Keith passed their booth, stopped, and turned around. "Hey, Coop!" he said, "what were you doing out our way Friday night?"

Coop lifted his head. "Out your way? You mean, at Nightmare Hall?" He frowned. "What would I be doing at Nightmare Hall?"

Milo laughed. He leaned his tall, bony frame against the side of the booth. "Well, I asked you first. I saw a light out my window, coming from the woods above the creek. Flashlight. Looked like you holding it. You lose something out there?"

"Wasn't me," Coop said, returning to his pizza.

Milo shrugged. "My mistake. Sure looked like you, though. Wearing a maroon jacket just like yours. High school football jacket with the gold hornet on the back. Not too many of those on campus, are there? See ya!"

Friday night, Shea thought, the night she'd gone to the creek to meet the whisperer. Milo had looked out his window and seen someone he thought was Coop. It hadn't been *her*. She didn't look anything like Coop, not even from a distance, not even in the dark. And she hadn't been wearing a jacket with a hornet on the back.

Did that mean the whisperer was someone who looked like Coop? Tall, broad-shouldered, dark, curly hair?

She knew that jacket. Coop was from Avalon, a really small town several hours from Twin Falls. Her high school had played his in basketball and football. And though she'd never seen Coop in it, she'd seen that jacket on lots of other people.

Were there other people from Avalon at Salem? If there were, Coop hadn't mentioned them, and he didn't hang around with them.

It had stopped raining when they left Vinnie's. Coop and Shea, who had arrived on the shuttle, decided to walk back to campus. The others drove back.

"I wonder who Milo saw at Nightmare Hall Friday night," Shea said casually as they made their way along the puddle-spattered road.

"Beats me. Why? I mean, why are you wondering?"

Shea wanted to explain. But how could she say. "Because I was there that night and I want to know who was in those woods with me?"

Still, if Milo was right about the jacket, and the whisperer was someone from Coop's hometown, it was probably someone Coop *knew*. How could she find that out without giving herself away?

She couldn't. "Just curious, I guess. I mean, don't you think that roaming around those woods late at night is a pretty weird thing to do? And speaking of weird" . . . should she really ask this? . . . "have you heard if the police know anything about who attacked Dr. Stark?"

"Nope. Not a word. I don't think they have anything to go on."

They crossed the road to campus. The tall pole lights along the walkways dripped remnants of the recent rain, their yellowish glow turning the waterdrops into liquid gold. "Are there very many guys from your graduating class on campus?" Shea asked.

"Not that I know of. A few, maybe. I haven't checked it out." He gave her a curious glance. "If it's the jacket you're wondering about, I don't even know where it is. I think I left it at the A.B.S. lab a while ago."

She could sense that he wasn't interested in talking about it any further. He seemed preoccupied. But he'd already explained that. The job in the lab.

Look who's talking! Shea reminded herself.

As if you can concentrate on anything besides the whisperer.

Well, at least she'd finally done the right thing. She had refused to cut off Tandy's beautiful hair.

Now there would be no more phone calls or notes. Maybe this was the end of it.

And tomorrow, she'd go to Dr. Stark and confess everything. She'd take her medicine, whatever it was. It couldn't be worse than dealing with the whisperer.

Shea was still thinking about the jacket Milo had seen at Nightmare Hall as she said goodbye to Coop and got in the elevator at Devereaux. Suddenly, without warning, the lights went off and the elevator vanished into abrupt, complete darkness . . . and jerked to an abrupt halt.

Chapter 12

Shea stood very still in the pitch-black elevator, listening to the sound of her own breathing.

She reached out for the control panel to her right. Since she couldn't see to distinguish which button was the door opener, she pressed all of them, one at a time.

Nothing happened. The lights didn't come back on, the elevator didn't move, and the door didn't open.

There had to be an emergency button, one that would set off an alarm and send rescuers rushing to free her from this dark, airless box.

Although she slapped her hand, hard, against every single button on the panel, no alarm sounded. Nothing happened. The elevator didn't move, and it remained as dark as an underground cave.

"I don't know what to do," Shea said aloud,

dropping her hand to her side again. The sound of her voice echoed hollowly in her ears. Finding the words oddly comforting, she repeated them, slowly and carefully. "I do not know what to do," as if it were a chant designed to ward off danger.

When her eyes had become accustomed to the darkness, she glanced around and, finding nothing that gave her any hope, looked up at the ceiling. Didn't people in the movies sometimes exit a stalled elevator through a trapdoor in the ceiling?

It was there, all right. A small, square-lidded opening.

But in the movies, the trapped person was either one of those superathletic types, or he had someone else in the elevator whose shoulders he could stand on to reach the trapdoor.

She was no Arnold Schwarzenegger.

And there were no extra shoulders in this elevator.

Shea did the next best thing. She screamed.

She screamed loud and long, the sounds beginning deep in her belly and gathering volume as they made their way up through her chest, her throat, and out her mouth, where they bounced off the walls and slammed against her ears.

Wincing, she clapped her hands over her

ears and continued to scream for help until her throat felt like it was bleeding.

But no one came to get her out. The door didn't slide open, friendly faces didn't smile in at her, saying, "Well, Shea, what are you doing in there?"

No one came.

Was the elevator soundproof?

She leaned against the wall, her arms wrapped around her chest, staring into the complete blackness. She waited. . . . It seemed like hours that she waited anxiously, chewing on her lower lip, nerves tingling, ears straining for any sign of approaching help.

None came.

When she finally realized that no one was coming to rescue her, panic took over. She threw herself at the door, her fists pounding against it. Hammering with all her might on the unyielding metal, kicking at it with her feet, she croaked in a hoarse, raw whisper, "Open, damn you, open!"

She was so lost in her fit of panic that when the lights suddenly came back on, she blinked, startled. The elevator lurched, jerked, and began moving slowly upward again. At first, Shea thought she was imagining the movement.

But she wasn't. It *was* moving.

She fell against the wall and let out a deep,

shaky sob of relief. When the elevator slid to a halt and the doors opened, she was greeted by a sea of anxious faces awaiting her in the hall.

Voices wanting to know if she was all right swam around her as she stumbled free.

"What happened?" she asked hoarsely, her vocal cords throbbing in pain, her knuckles scratched and raw.

"Electricity went off," a tall boy in shorts told her. "Nobody knows why. Back on now, though," he added unnecessarily.

"We heard you screaming," a red-robed girl named Molly said. "But with the electricity off, there was nothing we could do. A couple of the maintenance men went downstairs to check it out. I guess they fixed whatever was wrong. You sure you're okay?"

Anxious to get to her room and collapse on her bed, Shea assured everyone that she was fine except for a sore throat from screaming, and left the group, half leaning against the wall as she went.

As she went, Shea wondered if it had begun raining again. Thunder? Lightning? A lightning strike nearby might explain why the electricity had gone off.

She listened for thunder, and heard none. No deep, rumbling growls from overhead.

Then why had the electricity failed, trapping her in that elevator?

Shea heard doors slamming behind her as everyone returned to their rooms. Why did her own room suddenly seem so far away? Miles and miles away from her, down the long, long corridor. And she had to walk it on legs that felt boneless.

She hoped Tandy was home, and awake. The need to tell someone about her horrible imprisonment in the dark, airless cage was overwhelming. Talking about it seemed like the only way to get *rid* of it. She would let every frightening moment spill out of her mouth and, once it was out, she could push it away and forget about it.

Maybe.

Tandy was home, but she wasn't awake. She was sprawled across her bed, still fully clothed, headphones on, Walkman lying beside her. She was sound asleep, her head half-covered by her pillow.

Shea sank down on her bed and curled up in a small ball. The window beside Tandy's bed was open, filling the room with the fresh, cool smell of recent rain.

She envied Tandy, so soundly asleep.

Shea lay awake, staring at the ceiling. Their room was small . . . but so much larger than the elevator. She could breathe again.

What if the electricity hadn't come back on? What if it had stayed off for an hour, or two, even three? What would she have done then?

Lost it totally, she admitted silently. No question. Another five minutes in that place and they'd have had to peel her off the ceiling when the elevator door finally opened.

Her eyes drifted over to the clock radio on her bedside table. It read nine fifty-three.

Except, of course, it couldn't be nine fifty-three. Because the electricity had been off.

How long had the blackout lasted?

If she didn't correct the time on her clock before she conked out for the night, they'd be late for class in the morning. She hated being late on Mondays. A terrible start to a new week.

As if having to confess wasn't the worst way in the world to start a new week.

Shea sat up and leaned on one elbow to reset the clock, using her wristwatch as a guide. Ten thirty-eight. She'd been in that elevator forty-five minutes.

It had seemed like years.

She was about to lie back down when the phone rang. Tandy never stirred.

Shea grabbed the receiver quickly to prevent another shrill ring. Maybe Coop or Dinah had heard about her being held captive by the elevator and wanted the details. It would be nice to talk to one of them. Then she might be able to sleep.

But it wasn't Coop's voice on the line. Or Dinah's. It was, instead, the familiar whisper, soft, hushed, so sly, so sinister. And the words it whispered made no sense. Even as Shea realized who was calling and her teeth clenched in sudden dread, the voice sing-songed its incomprehensible message in her ear.

"Shave and a haircut, two bits!" Click.

Shea knew the ditty. When she was small, with hair falling almost to her waist, her grandfather had sometimes teased her by singing the jingle while making scissoring motions with his hands, pretending he was going to cut off her hair so her grandmother wouldn't have to braid it anymore.

"Shave and a haircut . . ."

A haircut. . . .

Was he . . . was he reminding her that he was angry with her? Because she'd refused to hack off Tandy's hair?

No. He wouldn't just *call* her. He'd . . . he'd *show* her how angry he was. He'd . . . he'd *do* something. Something nasty.

"Shave and a haircut . . ."

Something nasty. . . .

Moving as if she were an old woman, Shea reached out and switched on the small blue lamp next to her bed. A vein at her temple throbbed visibly as her head turned slowly, slowly. Her eyes, wide with dread, scanned Tandy's sleeping form, saw nothing frightening or weird. Moved away from Tandy, along the bed, then down, over the side . . .

And there it was.

On the floor.

A round pool of yellow, like melted butter.

Tandy's hair.

Tandy's beautiful, lemonade-hued hair, thick and silky and curly, was puddled on the floor beneath the bed.

And Tandy slept on, unaware.

Chapter 13

Shea gasped. One hand flew up to keep any louder sound from spilling out of her mouth. No, oh no, he couldn't have, he *couldn't* have . . .

But he *had*.

Shea's lips formed a small, round "O" of horror. If Tandy awoke and saw that splotch of yellow lying on the floor . . .

Shea switched off the lamp and the room disappeared into darkness, taking with it the sickening sight of Tandy's shorn hair.

But it was still there. Waiting for Tandy to awaken and see it . . .

Shea slid backward on her bed until the wall stopped her flight. Pulling her comforter up to her chest, she sat huddled in the corner, staring wide-eyed, fighting tears. Her lower lip quivered, and she had to bite down on it, hard, to keep it still.

She knew exactly what had happened. The scene played itself out in her mind as clearly as if she were sitting on her bed watching it happen:

Tandy comes back to an empty room. She's glad to have it to herself. She doesn't lock the door because she knows Shea will be coming in soon.

Tossing the clothes she was wearing onto the floor, Tandy slips into a long white T-shirt and sits on the edge of her bed brushing her long hair fifty strokes, a ritual she never skips, no matter how late she arrives home. Then, humming softly to herself, she washes her face and brushes her teeth.

She spends a few minutes writing in her diary. Then she slips a tape into her Walkman, dons headphones, and flings herself across her bed on her stomach.

She is asleep in minutes.

Shea shivered and yanked the comforter up to her chin, her fists clutching the edges so tightly, her knuckles ached.

The movie in her head continued.

Tandy has been asleep for a while when the electricity goes off. The clock radio stops and the lighted lamp on Shea's table goes out.

The room is dark.

But Shea can still see everything perfectly,

as if the room were bathed in daylight.

The door opens. A figure moves inside, quickly, quietly, an air of stealth about it. Of course. Because it shouldn't be in this room. It doesn't belong. Tandy is asleep, unaware of the sneaking, slithering figure. Meanwhile, Shea is being held captive in a dark, stuffy elevator, so she can't come to Tandy's aid.

I *would* have, Shea thought miserably, tears pooling in her eyes. I would have stopped him if I could have. But I couldn't.

The figure is holding something shiny in its right hand. Something shiny and silver is being lowered toward Tandy's sleeping form. It looks . . . it looks sharp, pointed . . .

A knife. A knife!

No . . . there are two blades, not one. And the two blades make a slicing noise against each other as they're wielded threateningly above Tandy's head.

Scissors. The thing in his hand is a pair of scissors.

Tandy doesn't hear the slicing sound. Tandy is asleep, and wearing headphones. The music is still playing in her ears, drowning out any sound made by the silvery, shiny scissors.

Shea wanted to stop it from happening. She strained forward on the bed, about to scream, "No, no, *don't!*" She bit back the shout only a split-second before it slid over her lips and hit the air, realizing that shouting would do no good now. Too late. The scene that was playing itself out in her head had already happened. It was over . . . and Tandy didn't even know yet that it had taken place.

He bends low over Tandy, the shiny, silvery blades in his right hand. He lifts the thick strands of pale yellow and begins chopping. . . . quickly, deliberately, chop, chop, chop. As each clump falls free of Tandy's head, it drops carelessly to the floor, until, in a brief few minutes filled only with the cold, slicing sound, the clumps form their soft round pool.

Tandy, asleep, perhaps dreaming, never feels a thing, never stirs as she's being shorn.

So quickly, it's over.

There is a deep, triumphant chuckle from the figure as it straightens up, holding the last chopped clump high in the air, like a trophy. Then that handful, too, drops to the floor.

The figure turns and leaves, closing the door quietly behind it.

Tandy sleeps on.

Shea did *not* sleep. All night long, as the shadows in the room deepened and darkened and then slowly faded, she sat huddled in the corner, the comforter to her chin. Her anguished mind tortured her with what-ifs . . .

what if she hadn't done this or that, what if she *had* done this or that, wasn't there some way she could have stopped the cruel attack on Tandy?

And it *was* an attack. He hadn't beaten Tandy, or stabbed her, or slapped her. But he had injured her just as surely.

And when Tandy saw what had taken place while she slept . . .

Shea groaned aloud, and closed her eyes.

When she opened them, dawn had crept into the room, lighting the hardwood floor with a grayish hue. Monday morning had arrived.

For one brief, hope-filled second, Shea allowed herself to believe that none of it had actually happened. Maybe she'd been asleep and dreaming a terrible dream.

But when she reluctantly sent her eyes to the spot on the floor beside Tandy's bed, there it was . . . a golden sun made of soft, thick rays of hair, curled into one another in a circle.

It hadn't been a dream.

Because anything seemed better than sitting on her bed staring blankly at the evidence of last night's cruel deed, Shea dragged herself up and out of bed. She took a shower, thinking, If only I hadn't been so desperate for a copy of that stupid exam. And as she dressed in a long gauze skirt and white peasant blouse, she asked herself, Why didn't I warn Tandy that some crazy person wanted her hair chopped off?

Something inside her snickered, are you kidding? Tandy would have thought you'd gone off the deep end. She'd think *you* were the crazy person.

Tandy groaned, wriggled, stretched, her eyes opening slowly, reluctantly. She winced as she rolled over on her side and a headphone jabbed against her ear. Pulling off the headset, she flipped onto her back, her eyes on the ceiling.

Shea sat on her bed, hands folded in her lap. Her heart was pounding so loudly in her chest, she half-expected Tandy to lift her head and say, "Cut out that awful racket, will you?"

Instead, Tandy said, "Did I ever tell you how passionately I hate Monday mornings? More than you hate bio, and that should tell you a *lot*."

At the word "bio," Shea's stomach rolled over. If she'd studied harder, if she'd hired a tutor, if she'd gone to Dr. Stark for help, the terrible moment about to happen — wouldn't have to happen.

If, if, *if*! What good did ifs do?

"I propose," Tandy said lazily, "that we go to the state legislature with a petition to abolish

Mondays. How does that sound? Just think," with a sleepy grin, "that would only leave *two* days of bio! You'll go for that, right?"

Without answering, Shea remained sitting stiffly on her bed, waiting. . . .

"What's the matter with you? Get up on the wrong side of the bed?" Tandy sat up. "And how come you're already dressed?" She glanced sideways, at her clock. "It's so early."

And then Tandy sat up. Shea watched her expression change as she noticed something felt different.

Tandy sat up straighter, and her left hand reached up to see what the problem was. . . .

As her fingers felt the back of her head, the expression on Tandy's face became one of utter confusion. Her fingers moved along the back of her neck, stopped in confusion, then moved rapidly, searching, seeking. . . . Her right hand flew up to join the left, feeling the chopped, ragged ends where there should have been long, silky strands.

Tandy's mouth fell open. Her eyes widened in shock and disbelief.

"Tandy . . ." Shea tried, then realized there were no words that would help. None.

Tandy's eyes, huge with bewilderment, flew to Shea's face. What she saw there jolted her up off the bed and sent her, barefoot, across the floor to the dresser mirror. In her haste, she failed to notice the puddle of yellow nestled below her bed. It could as easily have been a discarded blouse or sweater.

Shea sat perfectly still, her heart aching as Tandy stood, in her long white T-shirt, in front of the dresser and confronted her reflection. She stared at it for an agonizingly long minute, turning her head to one side, then the other.

Then her mouth opened in a soundless scream.

Chapter 14

As Tandy took in the whole, horrifying picture of what had been done to her, her body went rigid. Her hands gripped the edge of the dresser as if she knew that without it, she would collapse. Her mouth remained open in disbelief. "No," she whispered, running her hands desperately over her head one more time, as if she might find that her hair had miraculously reappeared, "oh, no, no!"

She whirled to face Shea with bewildered eyes. "What's going *on*?" Tandy cried. "What's *happened*?"

Shea remained miserably mute. She spread her hands helplessly in front of her. Before she could think of something to say, there was a knock at the door, it opened, and Dinah stuck her head in, saying, "I thought I heard you guys . . . omigosh, what's wrong with your hair, Tandy?"

Tandy burst into wild tears and ran to her bed, flinging herself across it, burying her head in her hands as she sobbed hysterically.

Dinah moved on into the room. "What *happened* to her?" she whispered to Shea.

Shea knew she had to say something. She couldn't just keep sitting there as if she'd suddenly been struck mute. "Someone . . . someone cut her hair off last night while she was sleeping. When the electricity was off and I was trapped in the elevator." She pointed. "There it is, on the floor. It was there when I came in."

"You were stuck in the elevator? I knew the electricity was off. Sharon told me. But she didn't tell me anyone had been trapped in an elevator. How awful! You okay?"

Shea nodded.

"You're not serious about her hair, are you?" Dinah asked, glancing at Tandy, wailing wildly on the bed. "Someone cut it off last night? What are you talking about? Who would do that?"

"I don't know," Shea answered honestly. She *didn't* know who the whisperer was.

"I don't get it," Dinah said slowly, sitting down on Tandy's bed and awkwardly patting Tandy's back, heaving with wild sobs. "You're telling me that someone walked in here last night and hacked off Tandy's hair? That's so crazy!"

Shea nodded grimly. "I know. But apparently that's what happened." She still couldn't believe it herself.

Dinah's round face registered total confusion. "But why? Why would someone do that?"

Shea clenched her fists. This was all her fault. She'd started it, by copying that exam. She'd never intended to hurt anyone, but there it was, that bright pool of yellow on the floor, and there was poor Tandy, crying hysterically on her bed.

This would all end when the whisperer no longer had anything to hold over Shea's head. She'd be free of him and his stupid, crazy cruelty. And he'd quit hurting other people.

She knew that unless she did something, he wouldn't stop with Tandy. He'd continue to demand that Shea do things, horrible things, and when she refused, he'd do them himself, knowing she'd feel responsible.

It couldn't go on.

"I might be able to fix your hair a little," Dinah offered the sobbing Tandy. "I've cut my own hair and my little sister's a couple of times. Sit up, Tandy. Let me see how bad it is."

Tandy, lying face-down, shook her shorn head vigorously.

Dinah had to plead for several more minutes before Tandy finally forced herself upright. Her face was swollen and tear-streaked, and her expression was one of total desolation. "Why would someone *do* this to me?" she wailed.

"Maybe someone was jealous of how beautiful your hair was," Dinah suggested.

"*Was!*" Tandy cried. "*Was* beautiful. Now, I look like a freak! I'm not stepping one foot outside this room looking like this."

"Oh, Tandy, don't be silly," Dinah said softly. "You can't give up living just because someone cut your hair. Give me a pair of scissors and I'll see if I can fix this a little."

"I have a pair of scissors," Shea said, getting up and going to her desk.

But the scissors weren't there. She searched every inch of the cluttered desk. No scissors.

Giving up, she turned away from the desk, trying to remember if she'd left them somewhere else. She was about to say, "I can't find them," when she realized that Dinah, sitting on the bed beside Tandy, was holding something up in the air, a puzzled expression on her face. "I was sitting on these," she said slowly, looking up at Shea. "They were here, under Tandy's blanket."

The scissors. *Shea's* scissors.

What were they doing on Tandy's bed?

Tandy and Dinah were both looking at Shea, Tandy's eyes accusing, Dinah's questioning.

Shea took a step backward. "Oh, come on, you don't think that *I. . . . ?*"

"Of course not!" Dinah said hastily. "I'm sure the person who did it saw your scissors on the desk and grabbed them, that's all."

But Tandy said in a voice hoarse from crying, "If someone came in here to cut off all my hair, don't you think they'd have brought their *own* scissors?"

Shea had been thinking exactly the same thing.

"Maybe they didn't come in here to cut your hair," Dinah said calmly, beginning to arrange the ragged ends of Tandy's hair with her fingers, trying to decide where she should cut. "Maybe they came in for something else . . . to see if your electricity was on, or to borrow something, maybe a flashlight." She viewed the crazily varied lengths of Tandy's remaining hair with doubt in her eyes. "This isn't going to be easy," she added, before returning to the matter of the scissors. "Some girl who's always been jealous of Tandy's hair came in for something else, and when she found Tandy asleep and the scissors right there on Shea's desk, she flipped out. I think that's what happened," Dinah said firmly. She began snipping carefully, one ragged strand at a time.

"I *hate* short hair!" Tandy wailed. "I've always hated it! I'm going to look like a brand-new baby bird!"

"You're going to look really cute," Dinah said in that same calm voice. "You never should have had so much hair. Your face is too small."

"Since when are you an expert?" Tandy said bitterly. Then she added angrily, "I'm going to the dean about this! I'm cutting bio this morning and going straight to Butler Hall. This isn't any different than being robbed."

Dinah and Shea nodded. "You *were* robbed," Shea agreed.

"I'll have to take your scissors with me, Shea," Tandy continued, her voice cool. "I mean, Dinah *did* find them in my bed. There might be fingerprints on them, besides yours and Dinah's, I mean."

She thinks *I* did it, Shea realized. Tandy really believes I cut off all her hair last night. How could she think that? And I can't tell her about the whisperer. She'd think I was a raving lunatic. So would Dinah. They'd never understand.

But then, who would?

"I'm cutting bio, too," Shea said, standing up. "There's something I have to do." The sooner she confessed to Dr. Stark, the sooner this nightmare would be over.

"You'll see, you're going to feel a lot more free with short hair," Dinah was telling Tandy as Shea left the room.

The building had come alive with the usual Monday morning hustle to get over the weekend and get back into gear for a week's worth of classes. It was never easy, and the sounds of the struggle filled the hallway. Cranky voices complained from behind closed doors, the pipes groaned with the strain of too many showers at the same time as residents of Devereaux fought to fully awaken, and typewriter keys raced to finish papers neglected over the weekend and due that morning.

When I first got here, Shea thought as she entered the elevator, I loved Monday mornings. The start of a whole new week always seemed like such a great thing. But then, I loved everything about Salem University at first, didn't I?

The elevator door had already begun to slide shut when Shea realized, with cold-sweat certainty, that she could *not* stay in this elevator. Not after last night. She hadn't been thinking when she got on or she would have headed straight for the stairs instead.

Her arm shot out and one panicky finger

pressed the DOOR OPEN button. With a huge sigh of relief, Shea jumped free.

Thanks to the whisperer, it would be a while before she could enter an elevator without panicking.

Because, although she wasn't sure *how* he was responsible for the blackout last night, she knew that he was. He'd probably found the master switch, wherever that might be, and turned it off before he sneaked into their room to hack off Tandy's hair.

Shea took the stairs down to the lobby.

It was empty and quiet there. The heels of her black flats click-clacked across the tile floor as she headed toward the big, double front doors. Her stomach writhed at the thought of facing Dr. Stark with the truth. How would the professor react? Probably turn her over to the administration immediately, with a demand for absolutely *no* clemency.

Probably not.

Dr. Stark had never been the friendliest, warmest person on campus. She'd probably be even worse after what had happened to her.

Maybe she wouldn't even listen to Shea.

But . . . I won't know until I try, Shea told herself, rounding a corner where the lobby wall jutted out at an angle, hiding from her view a small alcove off to her left. The alcove held only a desk with brochures on it, a worn plaid couch, and a door leading to the basement.

Shea heard no sound, saw nothing. One minute she was almost to the door, and the next an arm had wrapped itself roughly around her neck and was dragging her backward, into the alcove.

"Well, good morning, Miss Goody Two-Shoes! Think you're too saintly to give someone a simple haircut, do you? That's pretty funny, coming from a cheat! And just where do you think you're going?"

Chapter 15

"*I said, where do you think you're going? Didn't suddenly decide to confess all, did you, Shea? Not a good idea. Not good at all.*"

The grip around her neck was so tight, Shea had trouble breathing. She had told *no* one that she was going to see Dr. Stark. How did he *know* that?

Reading her mind, he whispered into her ear, "*I just guessed. You look like a woman on a mission. Forget it. You're in even deeper trouble now than you were before. Poor little Bethany could have died, and it would have been your fault. Sorry about that. How was I supposed to know she had a bad heart? It was Annette I was really after.*"

"Where's the tape?" Shea gasped, her fingers clawing at the arm around her neck. "You promised! I'm not doing another thing you ask me to. You might as well give me the tape now."

"Maybe you're right."

Shea's heart jumped. Did he mean it?

"Tell you what. If you can find the tape, you can have it." Soft, wicked laughter. *"I tossed the paperweight into the river. It was a nuisance dragging that thing around. It's heavy, you know? But the tape can still hang you. Here,"* something was thrust into her shoulderbag, *"maybe this will help. Don't say I never gave you anything. But if you don't find the tape, you're still at my beck and call."*

Before she could gasp an answer, the arm was released from around her neck. The door behind her opened and closed with a sharp click, and she was alone again.

Relief flooded her body as she rubbed her raw throat with one hand. He was gone. And he hadn't threatened her or made her promise to do something disgusting for him.

He had given her something . . . stuck it into her shoulder bag. What was it?

She sank down on the worn plaid sofa in the alcove and pulled her bag onto her lap. She thrust a hand into its soft folds, and almost immediately, her fingers closed on something that hadn't been in there before.

A cassette. But not the tape she wanted.

This was an audiocassette. A message from the whisperer? Her heart sank. Maybe the reason he hadn't assigned her some miserable task while he was choking her was, he'd already put it on tape. Maybe this cassette contained new instructions for her, some gruesome new task . . .

But he'd *said* she could have the videotape if she found it. Did he mean it? How would she know where to begin looking?

She didn't have a Walkman.

But Tandy did.

Sighing heavily, Shea forced herself to her feet and reluctantly made her way back up the stairs to the fourth floor.

When she walked into the room, Dinah was curling Tandy's new, short hairdo with a curling iron.

"I thought you guys would be done by now," Shea said, disappointed. She *had* to listen to that tape.

"Dinah went to get her curling iron. Took her forever," Tandy said. "I've already missed bio and now I'm missing English."

"Get your priorities straight," Dinah cautioned, deadpan. "What's really important here, an education or your hair?"

Tandy was still too upset to laugh.

Impatient with both of them, Shea asked

abruptly, "Tandy, can I borrow your Walkman for a minute? I've got a new tape I want to check out, make sure it's okay."

Dinah looked up, dark brows furrowed. "You went out this early in the morning to buy a tape?"

"No. It was . . . in my mailbox. My brother sent it. Tandy?"

"Sure. Help yourself. It's right there on my table."

Taking the Walkman, Shea donned the headphones and went into the bathroom, closing the door behind her. She didn't care if they thought she was acting weird. The only thing that mattered now was finding out if the whisperer had given her another crummy "assignment," or if he'd meant what he said.

She sat down on the cold, tile floor. By accident, she pressed the RECORD button first, but quickly caught her mistake. She pressed PLAY and leaned back against the wall.

Go directly to the house of nightmares.
Enter.
Beyond those doors lies your answer.
If you find what you seek, do whatever you will with it.
If you fail, the prize remains in my keeping.
And you will do my bidding without

question.

Find it or be sorry.

The tape clicked off.

Shea remained on the floor, motionless, confusion in her face. *The house of nightmares?*

Nightmare Hall.

The tape was hidden at Nightmare Hall?

But . . . how would she find it? She'd never even been inside the creepy old house.

She played the tape again, hoping there would be more on it than what she'd already heard. But that was all there was.

She would never be able to find that videotape. And there was a party there that night. She couldn't very well go searching through the place with people all around her.

But . . . what choice did she have?

She could still go to Dr. Stark and confess. But the thought terrified her.

And now . . . she had this one, tiny chance. The paperweight was gone . . . Now, all she had to do was find the tape, and she'd be free of the whisperer and free of the threat of expulsion. She'd destroy the tape, and that would be the end of it.

Now all she had to do was figure out where the tape was hidden . . .

Chapter 16

That night, while they got ready for the party, Shea tried to casually pump Tandy for information about Nightmare Hall: How big was it inside, how many rooms, how many floors?

But Tandy was so preoccupied with the favorable reception her new hairstyle had received on campus, she couldn't concentrate on anything else. "For heaven's sakes, Shea, why are you asking me all these questions about that place? Afraid you'll get lost?"

Shea forced a laugh. "Well, yes, actually, there are lots of other place I'd rather be lost."

"It's not that bad." Tandy slid a pink silk tank top over her head, careful not to mess up her new hairstyle. "It's just old. Haven't you ever been in an old house before?"

Shea asked no more questions, afraid Tandy would get suspicious. She'd just have to wing it when she got to the house.

"Oh, I almost forgot," Tandy said, picking up her purse, "Coop called while you were in the shower. Just wanted to make sure you were going to be there tonight." Her eyes narrowed. "I said no, but that *I* would be, and he was going to *love* my new hairstyle."

"You did not," Shea said calmly, sliding her feet into black flats.

"No, but I could have. Don't forget, I saw him first." Tandy's voice hardened slightly. "Then he asked to be introduced to *you*."

Shea stopped brushing her hair and looked at Tandy carefully.

Tandy laughed and waved a hand in dismissal. "Oh, well, what's one more cute guy in this world so full of cute guys? Now, hurry up. I can't wait to stun everyone at the party with my gorgeous new look."

They were almost to the elevator when Shea stopped and said abruptly, "Go on ahead. I forgot something."

Tandy frowned, but went on.

Shea went back to the room, picked up Tandy's Walkman from her table, inserted the cassette tape the whisperer had given her, and slipped the Walkman into her shoulder bag. If she was going to go into an unfamiliar house looking for something, she might as well take the only clue she had. She had no idea how or even *if* the Walkman would be helpful, but having it in her possession felt, somehow, useful.

Then she hurried out of the room and down the fire stairs to catch up with Tandy.

Nightingale Hall was every bit as threatening-looking up close as it seemed from afar, Shea decided as Sid's car crunched along the graveled driveway leading up the hill.

Tandy complained loudly during the drive about the dean's reaction to her haircut. "She said she was sure it was a prank! Can you believe it? A prank! As if we were in sixth grade. She said I could file a formal complaint if I insisted, but I could tell from her voice that no one would pay any attention to it."

She was still loudly deploring the "lack of security" on campus when Sid turned into Nightingale Hall's driveway.

The huge, off-campus dorm at the top of the hill was aglow with lights. But somehow they did little to dispell the creepy atmosphere.

Shea forced herself to "mingle" for the first half hour, as if she really had come there to party. She talked to people, laughed at all the right moments, pretended to sip her drink and nibble on a taco, but all the while her eyes were sweeping whatever room she happened to be in, looking for some clue.

If I were a videotape, where would someone hide me? she asked herself repeatedly, never coming up with a satisfactory answer. There were so many rooms in the house—living room, a library filled with floor-to-ceiling bookshelves, a long, narrow kitchen at the rear of the house, a big dining room, hallways, pantry and closets, and a curving wooden staircase leading to the second floor. There was also, she had been told, a basement and an attic. How would she ever cover that much ground by herself?

Disheartened, Shea almost gave up then. It was impossible.

It was Coop who inadvertently changed her mind. He arrived late, slightly breathless. When he spotted Shea sitting on the piano bench, he came straight toward her. "Sorry I'm late," he apologized. "Made the mistake of getting caught up in a movie in the Student Center, and wanted to see how it ended. I think you'd like it. Maybe I'll rent it some time and we can watch it together."

Rent it . . . watch it . . . on . . . a VCR! Shea smiled broadly at Coop. That could be *it*! If I were a videotape, she told herself with satisfaction, I'd be hiding in a VCR.

"Excuse me," she said to a baffled Coop, "I'll be right back." Jess Vogt, who lived at

Nightmare Hall, was standing at the dining room table, filling a paper plate. Shea forced herself to walk up next to her, pick up a plate and say as casually as possible "So Jess, do you guys have a VCR here?"

"No, we don't," Jess said. "Why?"

Shea shrugged, "Oh, I was just wondering . . ."

"Mrs. Coates has one, though," Jess continued, moving around the table as she filled her plate. "Our housemother. She doesn't go out much, so she rents a lot of movies."

A surge of renewed hope flowed through Shea. The housemother! She had a VCR. Where did she keep it?

"It's in her room," Jess said, as if she'd heard the question, "and sometimes she invites us to watch a movie. But she has that small bedroom off the kitchen and there isn't room for more than one or two people at a time."

Shea registered the information carefully. Small bedroom off kitchen. Okay. Now, she decided, the best thing to do was keep making conversation and filling her plate. Then she would walk away, set the plate down somewhere, and sneak into the kitchen to find that bedroom and, she hoped, that tape.

Coop would be looking for her. She hurried back to him, handed him her plate, saying,

"Here. Eat hearty. I'll go dig up some drinks somewhere. In the kitchen, I guess," and turned and left before he could say a word. Checking to make sure the housemother was not in her bedroom — she wasn't, she was in the dining room filling several bowls — Shea slipped along the hallway to the kitchen. She wouldn't have much time. Any minute now, Mrs. Coates would be returning to the kitchen and then might retire for the evening to her room. Every second counted.

Shea opened the pantry door by mistake. But the second door she tried was unlocked, and opened to a small, cluttered bedroom with a neatly made bed covered with a chenille spread, an old, dark dresser, squat, ugly chest of drawers, and, against the wall opposite the foot of the bed, an inexpensive wooden cart holding a television set and . . . a VCR.

Shea glanced back into the kitchen. No Mrs. Coates yet. She closed the bedroom door softly, and hurried over to the cart.

She touched the eject button on the VCR, and a tape slid forward. Was it the one?

Shea grasped the tape and looked for some identifying label. There it was, on the side, in black ink. STARK OFFICE.

How on earth had the whisperer gained

access to this room in this house?

Maybe it hadn't been so difficult. The house would have been empty most of the day, with everyone in classes or in town buying supplies for the party. It might not have been that difficult for someone to slip in, plant the tape, and hurry away.

Shea slid the tape into her shoulder bag. No time to look at it now. She'd never dare view it in this room. She had to leave *now*, before someone found her in here.

There was always the lounge when she got back to Devereaux. If she waited until everyone else had gone to bed, she'd have that VCR all to herself.

I've waited this long, what's a few more hours? she thought. She *had* the tape. It was hers. She wasn't going to have to confess after all, wasn't going to have to face Dr. Stark. She could stay in school and never do anything so stupid again, as long as she lived.

"What are you doing in here?"

Shea whirled, furious with herself for not leaving the room more quickly.

Dinah was standing in the doorway. Sid, Tandy and Coop were behind her.

All four were looking at Shea as if they'd caught her stealing Nightmare Hall's silverware.

Chapter 17

"I . . . I got lost," Shea said, moving away from the VCR. She was almost positive the tape had been safely hidden in her shoulder bag before they all arrived on the scene. "I thought this was the bathroom."

"The bathroom's upstairs," Tandy said, her voice cool.

She still thinks I had something to do with her haircut, Shea realized with a stab of resentment.

"You walked all the way across the room before you realized this wasn't the bathroom?" Sid asked caustically. "Didn't the bed give you a clue?"

Shea's tone was defensive as she answered, "I thought maybe that door over there," motioning toward what she knew perfectly well had to be a closet, "was the bathroom."

"Right," Sid said sarcastically.

Shea sent him a look of disgust. What did he think she'd been doing, stealing the housemother's jewelry?

It didn't matter what he thought. She had the tape. If it hadn't been for the Tom and Jerry cartoon, she'd trash the tape right now, toss it in the kitchen garbage can, be done with it. But she *had* to see it first, make sure it was what the label said it was.

"Dance with me, Coop," she said, hurrying out of the room and tugging on his hand.

"I thought you were looking for the bathroom," Sid reminded her.

"I'd rather dance," Shea said lightly, and pulled Coop away from the group.

Now that she had the tape . . . *if* it was the right one . . . maybe she could relax and have a good time. She had to wait until later to get to the VCR in the lounge, anyway. Might as well enjoy the party.

She did enjoy it. After one or two dances with Coop, she was able, with some effort, to convince herself that she *did* have in her possession the tape that could have ruined her life. Convincing herself of that allowed her to relax and have fun.

But by the time she left the party with Coop, she was beginning to feel anxious. What if this wasn't the tape? What if the whisperer had tricked her again? What if . . .

"Is it me?" Coop asked when they were settled in the front seat of his car. He started the engine and steered down the long, gravel driveway. "You've been out in left field for the last fifteen minutes."

"I'm sorry. I've just got a lot on my mind, that's all."

When Coop had dropped her off at Devereaux, she ran down to the lounge, hoping it would be empty.

It wasn't. A group of Sylvester Stallone fans had taken over the room, apparently enjoying a marathon of the star's movies. When Shea asked how many more they were planning on watching, the boy she asked pointed to three more cassettes stacked on top of one another next to the television set.

She left in disgust. She *had* to look at that tape tonight.

Dinah was just going into her room when Shea came out of the stairwell.

"You looked like you were having a good time," Dinah said, moving toward Shea. Her tone seemed wistful.

"Didn't you?" As if anyone could have a good time with Sid-the-grouch.

"It's this stupid competition for the A.B.S. lab job," Dinah complained. "Sid isn't himself."

If only that were true, Shea thought. It would be a refreshing change. "Don't worry about it," Shea said. "There's nothing you can do to get that job for him."

"I know." Dinah's tone was unhappy.

The last thing in the world Shea wanted was to discuss Sidney Frye. "Listen," she said lightly, "do you know anyone who has a VCR? My mom sent me a tape from home, and I'd really like to watch it tonight. Kind of homesick, you know?"

"Your family sure sends you a lot of tapes."

Was that suspicion in Dinah's voice? "Well, do you? Know anyone who has one?"

"They have a couple at the library. Downstairs. In those cubicles."

Shea looked at her watch. It was quarter to twelve. She'd have to hurry before the libary closed.

"Great. See you later. Thanks." Shea's heart began pounding rapidly. She had almost given up hope of viewing the tape that night. The thought of waiting to find out if she really was off the hook had been sickening. She turned and ran back down the stairs.

The library was nearly deserted. A couple sitting at one of the long, wooden tables stood up as Shea entered. She didn't see anyone else. One librarian stood at the checkout desk. She frowned with annoyance when Shea entered. "We're about to close — "

"I'll just be a few minutes," Shea called, and ran down the curving iron stairs to the lower level before the librarian could stop her.

It was deserted. There was no one at any of the computers, no one using any of the VCRs in the little cubicles. Quiet as a tomb, and not very well lit.

After checking each cubicle, Shea went back to the first one and entered, closing the door after her. Her fingers trembled with anticipation as she inserted the tape and switched on the machine. Then she sank into the straight-backed wooden chair facing the VCR.

The picture wasn't that great. Unfocused. Dr. Stark still had a thing or two to learn about technology. In a corner at the bottom of the screen was the time and date. It *was* the day she'd been in Dr. Stark's office, the first time, when she'd copied the exam. But the time was an hour earlier than her visit. She would have to fast-forward. The librarian upstairs wouldn't wait forever.

There . . . the tall, potted plant, the heavy wooden desk . . . the pile of papers. . . . Shea felt a mixture of relief and elation. It really was the right tape, after all. And *she* had it!

She was free. Free of the whisperer and his tormenting. She could hardly believe it. At last!

She was about to fast-forward when a figure appeared on the screen. A pair of hands began fumbling frantically through the papers. But . . . the time on the bottom of the screen had only moved ahead a minute or two. It was still too early. Shea hadn't been in the office then.

And . . . Shea leaned forward . . . there was something else wrong . . .

The figure wasn't wearing jeans, a T-shirt, and a cardigan. It was wearing a university sweatshirt. And a pleated skirt.

"I don't own a pleated skirt," Shea said aloud.

But then . . . she didn't have short, dark, curly hair, either, did she? And she wasn't at all round. She was thin and angular.

"That's not me," she murmured, standing up to peer more closely at the screen.

There was a sound behind her as the door opened.

Shea turned.

"Well, I see you found it," Dinah said. She leaned against the door frame. Her face was very pale. "Good for you."

Chapter 18

"Found it?" Shea echoed.

"The videotape. From Stark's office." Dinah remained in the doorway, arms folded across her chest. "I thought you probably had. Why else would you be looking for a VCR?"

Struggling to get her thoughts in order, Shea turned and ejected the tape. She held it in one hand and turned back to Dinah. "You . . . that's you on this tape," she said slowly. "Going through Dr. Stark's papers."

Dinah nodded. Her face was still as white as the wall behind her. Her dark eyes never moved from Shea's face. "I know. Give it to me."

Shea's grip on the black plastic case tightened. "You were in the office that day, too? Before me? Looking for the exam?"

Dinah let out a deep breath and relaxed against the doorway. "I've been cheating in school for years. Ever since tenth grade. After a while, I couldn't remember when I hadn't cheated. It started with just one little math test. I was having trouble, and my folks were on my back every second. 'A *B* just will not do, Dinah, dear,' 'We know you can do better, Dinah, *dear*,' 'We do expect to see your name on the honor list, Dinah, dear.' They never let up, not for a minute. A friend of mine had stolen an exam, and he told me how easy it was."

A friend? Shea knew immediately who the "friend" was. Sid. And she finally understood why Dinah put up with Sid, who was too possessive and too critical of her. Because he *knew*. He knew she cheated. And just as the whisperer could have ruined Shea's life, so could Sid ruin Dinah's. If she made him mad. If she rejected him. If she gave him any reason at all, Sid could pull Dinah's college career, her life, down around her in ruins.

"Sid," Shea said.

Dinah nodded again. "I went away to music camp the summer after our junior year, and I met this really nice guy." Her eyes closed. When they opened again, she said, "I came home and told Sid I thought we should date other people. He went crazy. He said . . . he said it would really be a shame if my parents and everyone at school found out what I'd been up to all that time, how I got my straight A's. He reminded me that the scholarship I needed for college would go to someone else if the truth came out. Without it, I wouldn't be able to go. Not," Dinah added bitterly, "that any college would have accepted me if I'd been expelled from high school for cheating."

"That rat!" Shea said heatedly.

"No." Dinah shook her head. "I deserved it. I knew better. I took the easy way out, and once I started I couldn't seem to stop. I tried, when I got to Salem. I told myself high school was behind me and I could make a new start. Without cheating. And I did try, Shea, I really did. But Stark's class was beyond me. I went to her a couple of times to ask for help and she just said, 'Perhaps you have no business in an advanced class, Miss Lincoln.' And Sid kept saying, 'Why are you making yourself crazy like this? Just do what we did in high school.' " Bitter tears filled Dinah's eyes as she shrugged and said, "So, I finally did."

"And Dr. Stark caught it on videotape," Shea said sympathetically. She was in shock . . . Dinah had cheated all through high school? But then, she herself wasn't in any position to judge, was she?

"Oh, that wasn't the first time I'd cheated in her class. I stole other people's homework and copied it. But this was the first time I'd ever gone to her office. She said that exam was going to count for forty percent of our grade, remember?"

Of course I remember, Shea thought dismally. It scared me to death.

"I *had* to do well," Dinah continued. "Copying the exam was the only thing I could think of. I didn't want to, but I was so scared I'd fail."

"Me, too," Shea said. Dinah looked so pathetic, guilt and shame written all over her face. Then a picture of Dr. Stark, lying on the floor of her office, blood on the back of her head, flashed into Shea's mind. How far had Dinah been willing to go to get her hands on that videotape after she learned that it existed?

And would she be willing to do the same thing now, if Shea refused to hand over the tape?"

There was only one door in the tiny cubicle. And Dinah was standing beside it.

She took two steps backward.

"Oh, Shea," Dinah said softly, a bleak expression on her face, "I didn't hit Dr. Stark on the head. I'm a cheat, but I'm not violent. How could you . . . ?"

"I'm sorry," Shea apologized. "But if not you, then who . . . ?"

"I think," Dinah said with great effort, "I think it was Sid. Maybe to protect me. I told him I was on that videotape. He knew how upset I was." Her voice softened. "He really does love me, Shea. In his own way."

Shea snorted in disgust.

"He probably went to her to plead my case, she got nasty with him the way she did with me, and he just lost it. All he told me was that he broke into her office when she wasn't there, to steal the videotape, and it was already gone. I almost went crazy. Then when she got hurt and the tape didn't show up, I thought Sid had attacked her, but I couldn't imagine where the tape was. Until . . . until I saw you at Nightmare Hall in the housemother's room, hanging around the VCR. That made me suspicious. Then when you asked me later who had a VCR, I was positive you had it. I didn't know why, though. I couldn't imagine you cheating, Shea. Then I thought maybe it was Coop who had cheated, because he wanted that summer job so much. I figured he was on the tape, too, and you were trying to protect him the way Sid had tried to protect me. So you stole the tape."

Shea didn't know what to think. If Sid was the one who had hit Dr. Stark on the head and left her on the floor of the office, was he the whisperer? Where had Sid been when she got those phone calls?

He'd been at Vinnie's, playing pool, that first night. He could have called her from the front telephone. She had no way of knowing where he'd been when she'd received the other calls. With Dinah, probably, but he could have slipped away for a few minutes in the lounge or the Student Center or a movie theater and made a quick phone call.

"Sid isn't good for you, Dinah," she said quietly. "He really isn't."

"I know. That's why I took the summer lifeguard job. I really didn't think Sid would get that lab job. I was sure Coop would get it. Dr. Stark couldn't stand Sid. So I figured Sid would have to go back home, and I wouldn't. I'd be free of him all summer long."

Shea moved forward to stand close to Dinah. "What if the two of us take this tape and go straight to the dean right now? I know it's late, but I have a feeling she'd see us if she knew how important it was."

Doubt filled Dinah's tear-streaked face. "To the dean? Oh, god, Shea, that means automatic expulsion! My parents would kill me!"

"Maybe not. We're confessing, right? That should count for something. And there just might be something on this tape the police can use to catch whoever attacked Dr. Stark."

Dinah looked confused.

"Come on, Dinah," Shea urged gently, "we have to do this. We'll both feel better. What do you say?"

"She says no way," a harsh guttural voice shouted. An arm in a maroon jacket reached in from beyond the door and shoved Dinah so hard, she fell against the doorframe, cracking her head sharply. Her knees gave way, and with a startled, "Oh!," she slid to the floor. Her eyes closed as she landed, her back against the wall, her head sinking into her chest.

Shea stared at her, so shocked that when the same arm reached in and yanked the videotape cassette out of her hands, she offered no resistance.

Uttering a cry of triumph, the figure in the maroon jacket, a gold baseball cap on his head, took off down the hall, waving the cassette in the air.

All Shea saw was a maroon and gold blur.

"Dinah?" she whispered.

Dinah remained motionless on the tile floor.

Shea glanced around desperately for a telephone. None. Were they all upstairs?

If she took the time to hunt for a phone, Dinah's attacker would get away.

She couldn't let that happen.

Taking one last, regretful glance at the unconscious Dinah, Shea ran from the room.

Chapter 19

The long, dimly lit hall was empty. Rushing from door to door, Shea hastily checked each cubicle. They were all empty, with no place for anyone to hide.

There was, she knew, a back staircase at the far end of the hall. Probably used for deliveries. Had he gone back upstairs?

She ran down the hall, and hesitated when she reached the foot of the staircase. Completely enclosed, narrow, it was very dark. No lighting. He could be hiding up there in the shadows, knowing she would follow him. Was she doing yet another stupid thing? Wouldn't it be smarter to go upstairs by the front staircase and tell the librarian to call the police?

But there was no time. If he got away . . .

Taking a deep breath, Shea ran up the stairs to the upper floor. Which was completely dark.

Either the librarian had forgotten Shea and Dinah, and closed up or . . .

Or the whisperer had taken care of her.

Shea stopped, afraid to move away from the door. She couldn't see. She couldn't breathe properly. She couldn't think.

Phone . . . where would the phone be? On the main desk, the big, wooden semicircular desk like a giant letter "C," in the middle of the room as you entered the library. If she could find it . . . over there . . . to her right, wasn't it?

Trying to picture what else was in the area, Shea began cautiously moving forward, one hesitant step at a time, feeling with her feet for any obstacle in her path.

"I didn't think you'd find the tape."

Shea froze.

The whisper came from somewhere above and to the right of her.

The balcony. Stacks and stacks of books up there. Another curving iron staircase led the way. An iron railing ran the entire length of the area. Old, leather or overstuffed chairs and reading tables were placed along the railing. Shea had always found it a cozy place to sit and study or read.

But not now. Now, it hid the whisperer.

"I didn't think you were smart enough to

figure out the obvious," the voice above her hissed. *"The tape in the VCR. If you're so smart, how come you were cheating? I saw you on that tape. It's more disgusting when smart people cheat. They're just lazy, that's all."*

Coward! Why didn't he come downstairs and face her instead of hiding in the dark and whispering? Sneaky, slithery little snake! Shea whirled around to face the balcony, lifting her head to shout, "You hurt Dinah!"

"She had it coming. She cheated, too. Although there's a little more excuse in her case. She isn't as bright as you are."

Shea had never been so angry. Frightened, too, alone in this dark, empty library with a sneaky, slimy, sick creep. But she was angrier than she was frightened. He had no *right* to play these stupid games! He had no *right* to hurt Dinah, to frighten Bethany and Annette, to attack a teacher, to chop off Tandy's hair. No right at all.

"Don't even think about the telephone. You'd never get there before I got to you. And you'd be sorry you tried."

He was always telling her she'd be sorry. She was sick of it.

She couldn't see him. But . . . that meant *he* couldn't see *her*, either. She bent at the waist to pull off her boots. Maybe she'd never make it out of this library alive. But before she gave up, she was going to find out who had been tormenting her for so long.

No matter what he said to her, she wouldn't be able to answer him as she made her way up the stairs. Speaking would give away her location. He mustn't know she was on her way up there. The only tool she had to use against him was the element of surprise. It wasn't much, but it was something.

There was a light switch at the top of the stairs, on her right, she remembered. If she could make her way to the top without giving herself away, she could hit that switch and flood the balcony with light.

She had no idea what she would do after that. But at least she'd know who she was dealing with.

"You're all alike, you cheats."

Shea bent to pick up one boot, gripping it tightly in her left hand by the top, so that the two-inch, stacked wooden heel swung free. Then she tiptoed to the stairs and put her foot on the bottom step.

"You want things the easy way. Don't want to have to work for them. Too much trouble. All you care about is having a good time, partying while the rest of us work to get what we want. You make me sick."

The second step, the third, the fourth . . . her breathing was too loud. He'd hear her. Did that last step just creak?

No. He was still whispering away.

"You think it's easy, always working so hard? You think the rest of us wouldn't like to take the easy way, too? But we're not like you. We know that cheaters are only cheating themselves."

The fifth step, the sixth . . . how many were there? She must be careful not to bump the railing, even brush against it . . . her sweater might make a rustling sound . . . alert him.

"Why don't you answer me? Cat got your tongue? Or are you too ashamed to defend yourself? You know I'm right, don't you, Fallon?"

The seventh, eighth . . . *why* was her breathing so loud?

She froze again halfway up the steps as he stirred, moved above her. *"Are you still down there?"* Suspicion in his voice. *"You couldn't have left. I would have seen the door opening. And you couldn't have called for help. I'd have heard you on the phone."* Silence. Then, with a note of uncertainty, *"Fallon? You there?"*

She had to hurry. If he moved away from the railing, decided to come downstairs and get her . . . he'd *meet* her on the stairs!

The ninth step, tenth, eleventh, hurry, hurry, but quietly, be *quiet*! Stop breathing, you idiot, just for these last few seconds, these last few steps. Then you'll hit the light switch, and you'll see who has been trying so hard to drive you over the edge.

The whisper, when it came, was louder, more insistent. She could practically feel all of his senses on alert. *"Fallon? Where are you? You're not down there, are you? Why don't you answer me?"* Then, heavy with suspicion, *"What are you up to?"*

The twelfth, thirteenth . . . she was so surprised to reach the top of the steps, she almost stumbled and fell against the wall. She held her breath as her right hand stretched out and felt along the wall, up, up, for the light switch . . . where *was* it?

"Fallon?" The whisper edged closer . . . he was moving toward her! *"Fallon, what are you trying to pull? I won't stand for any nonsense, do you understand that? I'm the one with the upper hand here. . . ."*

Her desperate fingers felt only the flat, smooth surface of the wall. Still, they kept searching, searching . . .

There! The switch, at last! If she didn't take a deep breath in the next second, she was going to pass out.

"Who do you think you're messing around with . . ."

Shea flipped the switch.

The balcony filled with light.

A shout of rage came from the figure in front of her.

It took Shea several stunned seconds to grasp who it was. The person was wearing a maroon football jacket . . . jeans . . . boots . . . baseball cap . . . no hair visible . . . but . . . if there *had* been hair spilling over the shoulders of the maroon jacket instead of tucked up under the baseball cap, it would have been, Shea knew now, almost the same color as hers. Something Dinah had pointed out that night at Vinnie's.

The same color, yes, but worn very differently. Not short and wavy and worn loose like her own, but pulled back from a thin, stern face into a severe, eyebrow-tugging knot at the nape of the neck.

And Shea realized something else. The person stood on two perfectly good legs.

It was Dr. Mathilde Stark.

Chapter 20

"Your legs . . ." Shea stammered, staring with disbelieving eyes at Dr. Stark.

The professor looked down with amusement. "Yes, they're my legs."

"But . . . but you're paralyzed!"

"Apparently not." The doctor pushed a leg forward, lifted it, wiggled her foot in its flat-heeled shoe. . . .

A shoe, Shea realized, very much like the shoes she had seen disappearing through a side door in the lounge the night the whisperer had hidden in the television cabinet.

No. Impossible.

"Be there or be sorry," the professor whispered, leaning casually against the black metal railing. The videotape was still in her hand. She smiled lazily, her cold blue eyes on Shea's face.

"You?" Shea gasped. Her hand was still on

the light switch. *"You?"* Her other hand held the boot. And, she remembered then, her shoulder bag held a tape recorder. With a tape in it. As nonchalantly as possible, she slipped her hand into her purse and pressed RECORD.

"So . . . who attacked you? I thought the whisperer had done it. But if *you're* the whisperer, then who . . . ?"

The professor laughed wildly, a cold, chilling sound that echoed throughout the balcony. "Oh, you stupid girl, there *was* no attack! No one hit me on the head. I lost a contact lens, and when I was crawling around beside my desk looking for it, I got tangled in the lamp cord and accidentally pulled the lamp and that stupid paperweight down on top of me. The lamp hit me on the back of my head, knocking me flat on the floor, and the paperweight was right behind it. Slammed me on the temple. I saw stars, and when I came to, *you* were in the room. I wanted to see what you'd do, so I played possum."

Shea's mouth fell open. "You . . . you were never attacked?"

"Well, of *course* I was . . ." another cackling laugh . . . "by my enemies, the lamp and the paperweight. The wretches hit me when I was down, you might say." Dr. Stark tilted her head. "Did I ever thank you for calling the emergency crew? No? Well, thank you, Fallon. I deeply and truly appreciate it."

Shea struggled to comprehend what she'd just been told. No attack? No one had hit Dr. Stark with the lamp or the paperweight? It had been an accident?

"You . . . you were conscious when I was in your office? And you deliberately let people think you were attacked? That doesn't make any sense."

"It certainly *does*." Dr. Stark began tossing the black plastic cassette from one hand to the other, as if she were playing catch with a ball. "I knew exactly what I was going to do the minute I woke up on that floor and realized what had happened. It was the perfect opportunity to teach you a lesson. I'd already looked at the tape. I knew you had been cheating." Her eyes narrowed. "Cheating *me*! You were *not* going to get away with it. I realized that if everyone thought I was paralyzed, I could do anything I wanted to, and no one would ever guess that it was me. So . . . I faked paralysis."

The look in Dr. Stark's eyes was chilling. Shea shrank backward, pressing into the wall. It was past midnight on a Monday night. Wouldn't Tandy begin wondering where she was? Maybe Dinah had awakened downstairs, found a phone down there somewhere, called the police?

Someone had better have done *something*. Because Dr. Stark wasn't going to tell Shea this whole story and then let her go. And there was that look in her eyes . . . if help didn't come . . . her only consolation was that the tape recorder, she hoped with all her heart, was recording this entire conversation. If anything happened to her, someone would at least find that tape recorder in her bag.

"You couldn't have fooled all those doctors into believing you were paralyzed."

"Oh, they couldn't find any reason for the paralysis. But I'd been traumatized by the attack. So they decided it was psychosomatic. But real, nevertheless. Actually, that worked out well. Had they thought it was my body turning on me, they'd have kept me in the hospital. Since they decided it was only my *mind*, they let me transfer back to campus, to the infirmary, which gave me the freedom I needed."

"The freedom to make my life miserable?" Shea asked bitterly.

"You've got it. The infirmary is so poorly staffed. And since I was no longer in any danger, they paid very little attention to me. When

I wanted to leave, all I had to do was have someone wheel me into the whirlpool and leave me there. I locked the door, insisting on my privacy. The first time I left by the back door, I had to borrow a nurse's uniform I found hanging in the closet. I picked up these clothes at the lab and from then on, when I went out, I was dressed as you see me now." She laughed. "So unlike me! Twice, I ran into people I knew, colleagues of mine. They never even blinked. Had no idea who I was."

"That's a horrible thing to do," Shea said with contempt. "Fooling everyone into thinking you'd been badly hurt, that you were crippled!"

The expression on Dr. Stark's face changed. She jerked upright, standing very straight and rigid, her thin, angled face cold and filled with hate. "And how dare you judge me? You stole an exam! Did you think I was going to let you get *away* with that?"

Trembling, Shea watched as Dr. Stark, her face red with fury, took a step forward.

There might not be much time left.

"What happened to the paperweight?" she asked.

"I shoved it under the bookshelves. It's still there. I didn't turn it over to the police because I wanted to handle things in my own way. I always say, if you want anything done right, do it yourself. Actually," she added, her voice cold, "that paperweight is going to prove very useful to me."

Shea didn't want to know how.

"Why Tandy?" Shea's fingers toyed nervously with the light switch. "Why Tandy's hair?"

"Because she's vain. She deserved to be taken down a peg or two. Good for her. Make her see what's really important. That girl, Annette, was just like Tandy. She wasn't here at Salem for an education. She was here for a good time."

"That's cruel. *You're* cruel," Shea said, unthinking. And then, so quickly that she didn't even know she had done it, her fingers hit the light switch, plunging the balcony into utter darkness.

Dr. Stark uttered an oath.

And Shea flew down the stairs in her stocking feet, rounded a corner so fast she smacked her cheek on the wall, kept going, flying down the hallway to the stairs leading to the basement.

She heard Dr. Stark behind her, muttering loudly, furiously, as she stumbled in pursuit of Shea. At first the rantings were unintelligible, but then the voice gathered strength and volume until it was almost shouting.

And Shea, racing down the iron stairs, heard, "All the same . . . all of them . . . vain, silly things, in college for a good time . . . just want to be pretty and cute and popular . . . don't know the first thing about hard work and dedication . . . well, I could tell them a thing or two, I could . . . work, work, work, nothing but work and study, work and study, no time for fun, no time to find anything sweet and precious, have to succeed, *have* to . . . but it's no fun, no fun . . . all work and no play makes Mathilde a dull girl. Dull, dull, dull . . ."

She was so close behind Shea, her breathing filled the air in the dark, narrow stairway.

When Shea burst out into the basement, she didn't know where to go. The cubicles . . . a mistake . . . no way out . . . she'd be trapped in there and Stark would find her . . . where? where could she hide?

Don't stay down here, she told herself . . . too easy to be trapped down here . . . go back upstairs . . . take the back staircase, the dark one, go back upstairs . . . if you hurry, there's a chance you can get to the phone and dial before she catches up.

"Cheaters . . . cheaters, all of them . . ." The voice behind Shea rambled on furiously, "and that stupid girl with all that long, pretty blonde hair . . . she had it coming . . . taught her a lesson, all right . . . she won't soon forget Mathilde Stark . . . fools, all of them, fools!"

Shea dashed down the hallway, not even taking the time to stop and check on Dinah. She didn't dare. Every second counted.

"I can't let you out of here!" the insane voice behind her screamed, "not now! I'm not done! I'm not stopping with you. Campus is polluted with cheaters. You were only the first. Wouldn't have been able to do anything about it if that contact lens hadn't fallen out and the lamp hadn't hit me. Perfect, just perfect. Worked out so beautifully. Can do anything I want . . . no one knows I'm not paralyzed. Only you, and you're not leaving here alive, I promise you that, Fallon. You might as well quit running."

Shea's mind raced, like her feet as she flew down the hallway toward the back stairs. Dr. Stark had been following her all night. She had planted the tape at Nightmare Hall when the house was empty, and then followed tonight to see if Shea found it. Must have heard her asking Dinah about a VCR. Followed her here . . .

What had she done with the librarian? Or had she simply hidden until the librarian, forgetting about Shea and Dinah, had left early?

No. The librarian wouldn't have forgotten

about them. Stark must have done something to her. . . . Shea drew in her breath . . . was the woman still alive?

The professor's voice changed, became instead of the shrill shout, a harsh, loud whisper. She was very close . . . not more than a few feet behind Shea.

"Cheaters only cheat themselves, they do, they do, my mother said so, over and over again, and I tried to tell her I couldn't do the work, I couldn't, it was too hard, someone had to help me, and she screamed at me that I had to learn to do things for myself, to work hard, work hard . . ."

Shea reached the dark, narrow back staircase and darted up it. She couldn't see a thing, no light at all, and behind her the whisper continued, close on her heels.

"She could have helped me, she was smart, had her doctorate, taught lots and lots of other people, but not me, oh no, not me, said I had to do it myself, it was hard, so hard, but I didn't dare use a cheat sheet the way Joey Farmer and Debbie Sorenson did all the time, because cheaters only cheat themselves, they do, my mother said so, and she knew everything. Smartest woman I ever knew. But she wouldn't help me. Why wouldn't she help me?"

Fingers clutched at Shea's left ankle as she

scrambled up the last few steps. Sharp nails clawed at her skin.

Suddenly Shea realized she was still holding her boot. She swung backwards with it, hard.

There was a pained yelp behind her and the fingers on her ankle let go.

Shea scrambled up the last few steps, emerged into the main floor of the library again, ran, gasping for breath, toward where she thought the semicircular main desk should be. Fell. Got up, ran again, reached the desk, slammed into it, knocking the breath out of her. Searched desperately for the phone. Found it, picked up the receiver . . .

And a strong, clawlike hand grabbed a handful of her hair and yanked her head backward.

Chapter 21

Screaming in pain, Shea dropped the phone, but her index finger pushed the "O" down before her right hand flew up to struggle against the iron grip on her scalp, while her left hand searched frantically across the surface of the huge desk for something, anything, to use as a weapon against her attacker.

A second strong arm wrapped itself around Shea's waist, pressing the breath out of her. *"You don't know what it was like,"* the harsh, insane whisper hissed into her ear. *"Always studying, always working, never having any fun. People thought I didn't want to have fun, they thought I actually enjoyed being a drone. I hated it! I still hate it! I wanted to have fun, but there was no time. And after a while, I didn't know how. I didn't know how, and that was something I could never ask my mother. Because, as smart as she was, that's one thing she never, ever knew. How to have fun. . . ."*

Fingers searching, seeking . . . there! Hard, metal . . . a stapler. Huge. Gigantic. A giant stapler.

Shea's fingers closed around the metal tool as the hand on her hair and the arm around her waist began dragging her backward.

"Here's what's going to happen. You knew you'd be found out . . . not only your cheating would be discovered, but the truth about your attack on me was about to be revealed when the police received an anonymous tip about the location of the paperweight with your finger-prints and bloodstains on it. You couldn't stand the thought of the disgrace. So you hid in this library until it closed and then you went up the stairs and climbed up on that metal railing and jumped off."

"I won't . . ." Shea gripped the stapler tightly as Dr. Stark, with an arm around Shea's waist, continued to yank her backward . . . "I won't jump. Never."

"Oh, of course you will. Didn't I tell you I was in charge here? You will do as I say, young lady!" Rueful laughter. *"Oh, no, I can't believe it, I just sounded exactly like Her. My mother. Exactly. Maybe the doctors were right. Maybe I do need a psychiatrist!"* More laughter, a cackle of glee. But the grip on Shea's hair and

around her waist remained ironclad.

"When I'm finished with you, I'm moving on to your friend, Dinah. She's even worse than you. I looked at her transcript . . . no way did that girl deserve straight A's in high school. Been cheating for years, I could tell. She's next, she's next . . ."

In one quick, rough movement, Shea lifted the stapler high over her head and brought it down hard, on Dr. Stark's head.

Dr. Stark's scream of pain rang out throughout the dark, empty library like the shriek of a wounded animal.

And the hands flew away from Shea, releasing her.

Gasping in relief, Shea ran.

She had just made it to the front door when two uniformed campus security police pushed it open and grabbed at her. Over their shoulders, she saw the blue light of their car, parked at the library entrance.

"Don't let her get away!" Dr. Stark shouted from behind Shea. "The girl attacked me. She's been holding me prisoner in here." Holding up a bloody hand, she approached the group at the doorway. "I am a respected member of this faculty, and this student must be arrested. This is not the first time she's attacked me. I've been protecting her, hoping to help her out, but I see now that's not possible. . . ."

Her voice drifted off then as she finally noticed the object that Shea was holding up triumphantly in front of her, like a cross before a vampire.

The cassette from the tape recorder.

Dr. Stark screamed in fury and flung herself at Shea.

Epilogue

They were seated in a booth at Vinnie's on a warm Friday night in May. The restaurant was crowded, the music loud, conversations lively.

"No whispering this time," Shea said, smiling at Coop. "No teacher sitting across the aisle from us, trying to paralyze us with her poisonous gaze. It feels good."

Coop nodded. "We won't have to worry about her for a while. The new bio prof told me she'll be in that hospital for a long, long time. So," he took Shea's hand in his, "how does it feel to be on probation?"

"Honest," Shea said, laughing ruefully. "It feels honest. I don't hate it."

"Me, either," Dinah said, nodding agreement. "You were right, Shea. Making a clean breast of things really helped."

"Yeah," Dinah's date, a tall, thin boy named Russ Thompson said, "but don't forget . . . the dean had to give you guys a break so you wouldn't sue the school. I mean, let's face it, having a crazed professor on the faculty is a public relations nightmare for any university."

"I thought they did a really good job of keeping things quiet," Tandy volunteered. Her hair was curled in soft waves around her head, like a cap.

She looks like a pixie, Shea thought, and she does look really cute. And the truth was, the haircut hadn't lessened Tandy's vanity one tiny little bit. Dr. Stark's "lesson" hadn't worked in Tandy's case.

But that was okay.

Because, in a way, it had worked for Shea and Dinah. Although Dr. Stark couldn't take all the credit . . . some of it they'd discovered on their own . . . they had both received the message, loud and clear.

Shea looked at Russ and thought how much better he was for Dinah than Sid had been. Sid had left Salem, and was heading home to work for his father.

"I'm glad you got the lab job, Coop," Dinah said. "You deserved it. You worked hard for it."

"Thanks, Dinah. And now I can quit mooning around and start paying attention to the really important things." He stood up and took Shea's hand. "And now, speaking of important things, Shea has some heavy-duty studying to do with her new tutor."

"Who would be . . . ?" Dinah inquired with a grin.

"Who would be me," Coop answered. "Ready, Shea?"

"Yes," Shea said, "I'm ready."

Return to Nightmare Hall
... *if you dare*

A soft rustling sound broke the silence around Varsity Pond. The couple sitting on the park bench, enjoying the soft spring night, thought nothing of it. An owl, left homeless when the old Peabody gym had burned, had moved into a hollow oak tree near the pond. Bird watchers from the biology I class kept an eye on the tree, hoping the bird was nesting.

The girl snuggled close as the guy she was with stroked her hair with gentle hands. His first kiss was soft, lingering.

A groan from behind them caused her to pull back, alarmed. A musty smell grew stronger, became rotten, like a skunk long dead.

The low growl sent shivers throughout the girl's body. Her chest squeezed, leaving her struggling to breathe. She wanted to scream, but no sound left her open mouth.

Before she could get to her feet, before they

could run, the beast roared, attacked, slashing out with long, razor-sharp claws.

Everyone had joked about the monster stalking students on the campus of Salem University. Everyone thought it was a prank by the Sigma Chis.

The couple could testify that the creature was no prank.

They had evidence that the creature was real.

They could put the rumors to rest.

If they lived.

About the Author

"Writing tales of horror makes it hard to convince people that I'm a nice, gentle person," says **Diane Hoh**.

"So what's a nice woman like me doing scaring people?

"Discovering the fearful side of life: what makes the heart pound, the adrenaline flow, the breath catch in the throat. And hoping always that the reader is having a frightfully good time, too."

Diane Hoh grew up in Warren, Pennsylvania. Since then, she has lived in New York, Colorado, and North Carolina, before settling in Austin, Texas. "Reading and writing take up most of my life," says Hoh, "along with family, music, and gardening." Her other horror novels include *Funhouse*, *The Accident*, *The Fever*, and *The Train*.